The Hamilton Heirloom

A Kosher Harbor Story, Book 2

Castiel Skull

This is a work of fiction. Names, characters, places, and incidents either are the product of the author's imagination or are used fictitiously. Any resemblance to actual persons, living or dead, events, or locales is entirely coincidental.

Copyright © 2024 Castiel Skull

Cover art copyright © 2024 Castiel Skull

Cover design by Luna Design

All rights reserved. The scanning, uploading, and distribution of this book without permission is a theft of the author's intellectual property. If you would like permission to use material from the book (other than for review purposes), please contact author.castielskull@gmail.com.

First Edition: June 2024

Library of Congress Control Number:

ISBN: 979-8-9868937-5-4

To my aunt, Penelope Hamilton. When I was younger, I was plagued with night terrors. And sometimes a nightmare leaves an impression on a child that can haunt them for a lifetime.

PREFACE

2007

"Can you keep a secret?" the old man asked his grandson. The man's face was wrinkled and his cheeks had sunken into themselves where the years had aged his face. The old man was almost completely bald. Only a thin dusting of white hair wrapped around the sides to the back of his head. He bared down into the young boy's eyes and did not blink. The little boy stared into the wild eyes of his grandfather. He knew he had no choice in the matter. What he had just witnessed scared him. Not like a jump scare like in a movie, but a frightful scene that shook the boy to his core. A scene that would haunt him for the rest of his life, however long that may be. It was childhood trauma at its best.

"Ok, Grandpa. I won't tell. Just like in the barn. I promise, I'll be a good boy. I won't say a word."

Winston Hamilton flashed his dentures and smiled a wicked smile, satisfied with his grandson's response. "You're a special boy, Melvin. Now come closer and watch how I do it. I can teach you too." Winston walked back around to the butcherblock countertop. He picked up the hatchet and continued chopping. The sound of metal cutting into bone sank deep into the boy's ears, penetrating his mind. Just as Melvin took a few steps closer to get a better look, the old man swung the hatchet down again. Blood gushed out and splattered onto the boy's face.

CHAPTER 1

Kosher Harbor was a hidden gem within the sands of time. The perimeter of the peaceful town was riddled with gigantic alpine ash trees so high that one would think they could touch the stars at night. The town had a population of two thousand, five hundred and eighty-nine (with even more secrets) and was split into five districts. The town itself was shaped like a jagged letter "M" and almost all of Kosher Harbor was surrounded by water. Each district within the town had its own classification: the lower-class, where crime rate was at its highest and the poorest citizens of the town lived, the business district, which held most of the businesses within the harbor, the middle-class, where average income household residents lived inside their various brightly colored painted homes, the seafood market, where the Hamilton's and many other seafood vendors conducted fresh fish trade for cash, and lastly, the upper-class district, where the wealthy and only the wealthy belonged.

The town's wealthiest family were the Hamilton's. The family prided themselves on being the original and most powerful family before the town was declared a town in the mid-1800s. The current head of the Hamilton estate was Winston. He was in his late fifties and on the verge of retirement. Winston met his wife, Sophie in the early 1960s, when she and her family were shopping at the fish market. The day they met, Sophie wore her blonde hair in a ponytail and was dressed in a pink blouse with white pants. She wore no makeup nor jewelry; her parents forbade it. It was her innocence that captured Winston Hamilton's attention. Sophie's family were passing by his family's fish stand the second time when he grew the courage to finally speak up. She blushed when he spoke to her, bringing color to her cheeks. And in turn it brought nothing more than desire to Winston's heart. They were both teenagers at the time, him only two years older than she. But Winston had a family secret and was uncertain how to tell his new infatuation. He was not afraid of Sophie going to the police once he would tell her. Rather, he was afraid of her judging him after learning his family's secret.

And so, the demon wanted nothing more than to persuade this newly acquainted angel. And if she refused him...

"I don't want to touch it, Winston!" Sophie screamed as he held a squirming worm between his finger and thumb.

He finally convinced her one day to sneak away from her parents to go out on a date with him. Fishing.

"It's just a worm. It's not going to bite you."

"It's gross! Won't you bait the hook for me?"

That's not how it works. If you're to marry a fisherman one day then you got to learn how to fish. How can I live up to my family's expectations and be the most prominent fisherman in all of Kosher Harbor and my future wife doesn't know how to bait a hook? I would be laughed out of the town if that were to ever get out. I can't risk it, Sophie. I have a last name to live up to. You got to do this. Please. For me?"

Sophie made a face but reluctantly took the slimy

worm in her own hand. The invertebrate wiggled freely in the palm of her shaking hand. Sophie took the worm between her fingers and with the other hand she held the fishing hook. She pressed the sharp tip into the worm and pierced its flesh, causing its guts to spew from the hole it had created in its body.

"Eww, disgusting!" Sophie screamed, dropping the hooked worm from her hand.

Winston clutched his stomach and let out a booming laugh into the air. The paddle boat rocked from side to side. Sophie shifted closer to the side of the boat and leaned over. She began rinsing off her hands in the water. Winston's laugh faded out to an end and he let out a sigh as he watched his new girlfriend clean her hands. If this is how she acted with hooking a worm, there was no way she could be his wife. If Sophie was to marry into the Hamilton name, then Winston would have to take his time training her.

CHAPTER 2

Winston Hamilton was taught how to fish by his father when he was just a young boy. And his father was taught by his father, and so on. It was easy to learn how to fish. Anyone could do it. And many within Kosher Harbor were fishermen to make ends meat. But no other family caught as many fish as the Hamilton's. And none were as large either. Many have tried, even gone as far as buying new boats and equipment. But they have all failed at trying to overtake the seafood market. No one understood how the Hamilton family was so successful at catching not only the most, but the *biggest* fish as well. Some assumed it was the location on their private property. Others assumed it was special bait. Both assumptions were correct.

"Good morning, Mrs. Hamilton," Jillian Parker said as she approached Sophie's Seafood Sensations, the largest fish stand at the seafood market, which was owned and operated by Sophie Hamilton and on the weekends when business picked up, her daughter-in-law, Evelyn. It was the same fish stand that Winston was working when they met as teenagers. Sophie insisted on adding a business name and being the face of the Hamilton business when she took the Hamilton last name.

"Good morning, Jillian. And please, call me Sophie. We've known one another for almost a year now. And since you moved here, you're one of my best customers!" Sophie replied with her arms wide open, as if she was giving Jillian a pretend hug. Sophie was good at pretending. She did it well. In reality, Sophie did not like anything about Jillian. Maybe it was the blonde highlights she had; they were obviously fake. Maybe it was her positive personality about life that bothered the older woman. Whatever it was, Sophie Hamilton hated Jillian Parker.

"Well, what can I say, my husband absolutely loves your trophy sized trout," Jillian said with a most sincere smile on her face. The same smile that made

Sophie want to slap Jillian right across her face.

Maybe Sophie hated Jillian because she had the perfect marriage. A marriage where Jillian probably didn't have to walk on egg shells around her husband and always pretend that everything is normal and perfect in their life. A marriage that wasn't built on secrets. A marriage where Jillian didn't feel unsafe when her husband was in one of his moods…

Sophie returned a fake smile. "Well, our fish is to die for, isn't it?"

"I think Mitchel fell even deeper in love with me the first time I cooked him fish, bought from you and Evelyn of course. And today is a special occasion. And what better way to celebrate the good news than with some trout? I would like your biggest catch today, no matter the cost." Jillian craned her neck, searching for the biggest fish.

"Excellent!" Sophie said, the corners of her thin lips curling up into a wicked smile. "I have the perfect catch for… what did you say the occasion was for again?"

Jillian beamed in total happiness. She was practically glowing. "I just found out that I'm pregnant," she answered, touching her stomach. "I'm going to break the news to Mitchel over dinner tonight."

Sophie gasped and grabbed a hold of her pearl necklace with the hand that was decorated with an oversized diamond. It was a great opportunity to show off the jewels that was on her hand and neck. She did it at least once a week to an unsuspecting customer; just to remind them that she's the richest woman in all of Kosher Harbor. "Congratulations! I'm so happy for you," her voice said going up an octave while wrapping an oversized trout in paper after weighing it.

The fish looked as if it could feed a family of four for an entire week. It was longer than her arm from finger to shoulder and excessively plump. Sophie finished packaging the fish and then turned her back on Jillian and secretly pulled a key from her pocket. She unlocked the padlock on a small crate that was sitting on a table behind her. She turned back around and handed Jillian a small glass jar with a cork, filled with a mysterious white powder. The jar had no label on it. "Sprinkle a little of this onto the fish before baking it. It gives it even more texture and it's high in protein. It's an energizer that's all natural with no side effects. I made it myself."

"Oh, ok. How much are you selling it for?"

"Please, just take it. We're friends after all. Since you and Mitch moved to Kosher Harbor, you've been one of my most loyal customers. No charge."

"Oh, thank you! Maybe this will help give me some energy. I think the pregnancy has already been making me tired these past few days. That's why I went to see Dr. Hanus in the first place." Jillian placed the corked jar into her purse and pulled out some cash to pay for the fish. "Keep the change for a tip," she said, handing the money over to Sophie.

"Dr. Hanus is one of our neighbors. We know him well. You and your baby will be in good hands with that man as your doctor. Are you wanting to have a boy or a girl? Have you already been thinking of names?" Sophie asked, snatching the bills from her outreached hand.

Jillian Parker placed her hand to her stomach again. "To be truthful, I hope we have a girl. I've always wanted a daughter. And if it turns out to be a girl, I'm naming her Sandy, after my grandmother."

"Isn't that sweet." Sophie said, wearing a fake smile across her face as she handed the oversized and overpriced trout over to Jillian.

"How's Evelyn and little Melvin doing?" Jillian asked.

Sophie's fake smile disappeared from her face in an instant. "She's fine. She should be here soon with another delivery. And Melvin is doing excellent. He makes such good marks in school. He's bashful at times but so very curious. And my husband is also doing well, thank you for asking."

"I'm glad to hear it. I guess I better head home now to start prepping this," Jillian said, struggling with the heavy fish.

"Well, be sure to tell Mitch I say hello. But maybe not tell him that I knew about little Sandy Parker before he did. Men can be so fickle and jealous sometimes, am I right? And I really must get on your side of the harbor for a visit one night."

"Please do, anytime. We're located at Pier Seventeen. But I really must get going now. I have so much to do!" Jillian said, struggling to wave her hand as she turned to leave.

Sophie waved goodbye to Jillian. The sun bounced off her large diamond ring and into her own eyes. Most people would find it strange to handle fish all day while wearing a diamond, but Winston Hamilton would have it no other way. He wanted everyone who bought fish from his family to know that Sophie was a taken woman. He bought her two diamond rings when they married. One to wear while she was at the market selling fish and one to wear everywhere else. Sophie ran her fingers along the strand of pearls that decorated her neck, her most prized possession that brought back many memories; memories that she would never forget; memories she *could* never forget, even if she desperately wanted to.

Sophie looked around to make sure no one was watching her. She turned around and locked the padlock on the crate again. No one could ever know what the white powder really was. Otherwise, her family would be ruined.

CHAPTER 3

The Hamilton's lived in a two-story colonial mansion that was built in the mid-1800s. The house was painted pure white, and just like the family's angling secrets, the property in its entirety and all assets were always passed down to the firstborn son. Being the firstborn son within the Hamilton bloodline came with many perks. Winston was the firstborn son and his parents raised him on wickedness, entitlement, and caviar with a silver spoon since the day he was born. Nothing good came from being born second.

Winston and Sophie's firstborn child was a boy and they named him Carter. They raised him the same way Winston was raised. Disciplined to keep the family secret and with a fake facade for the public eye. The only problem with Carter was Evelyn. Once they met, he changed. He desperately wanted to keep her away from his parents. But Winston and Sophie wouldn't have it. They forced him to introduce them to the woman their son was in love with. She wasn't unnaturally beautiful like Sophie was in her younger years. Her family wasn't wealthy and she possessed no useful talents. She had no business being with their son. But it was too late. The day Carter introduced Evelyn to his parents was the day Winston and Sophie found out that Evelyn was carrying their grandchild. Hamilton blood was growing inside her womb and that made her family. A shotgun wedding was put together within a week.

Soon after the wedding, tragedy struck. Carter went out to sea and never returned. His boat was found by sonar, at the bottom of the dark waters. Something had torn the boat apart. No signs of a body were ever found. At least, that's what Evelyn was told.

"Just because you married our son does not mean you get to inherit any of this, young lady!" Winston barked at his daughter-in-law after it was mysteriously declared a shark had taken her husband's life while she was newly married and pregnant with their son. "After the funeral is over, we will never speak of Carter again."

Evelyn did as she was told. She learned the Hamilton secret the day after her wedding. There was no turning back. But Carter had promised her they would escape and start a new life; a good life for their son, Melvin. A promise he wasn't able to keep. She knew what would happen if she disobeyed her in-laws. It was then that Evelyn became evil out of fear, like most of the women that married into the family. But deep inside, Evelyn wanted to be good. She still wanted to escape Kosher Harbor and take her son with her, away from Winston and Sophie, forever. But with Carter passing away she was forced to rely on the Hamilton's to support her and her son. She owned no assets and had no money. She was a widow without a web.

Six months later, after her husband's death, she gave birth to a boy and was forced to name him Melvin, after Winston's own father. She tried to keep him away from Winston and Sophie as much as she could but it was difficult to do, seeing as they all lived under the same roof. She did not want Melvin to be like his grandparents, or even herself for that matter. Melvin was eight years old now. It was Hamilton tradition that once the firstborn son hit puberty, he was to help with the family business. Evelyn had been stashing money away in order to escape Kosher Harbor and raise her son away from this wicked town. She decided she would escape as soon as the opportunity presented itself. There was no way she would let her son grow up into becoming like his wicked grandparents.

CHAPTER 4

"Welcome to Kosher Harbor Elementary," the receptionist spoke to Winston as he entered the front office. "Please sign in on the clipboard and have a seat, Mr. Hamilton. Principal Harper will be with you shortly. He's with another appointment right now, but should be finishing up momentarily."

The old man sat down on the wooden bench, much too short for his height, that was stationed against the wall. He knew getting back up would be a struggle. And of course, right when he crossed his legs, the principal's office door swung open.

"Thanks again for volunteering, Mr. Tucker. This fish fry is going to be the best one yet. God knows we need this after the destruction of Hurricane Candi last year.

"It's my pleasure. See you next Friday!" Maverick Tucker said, noticing Winston sitting on the other side of the office. Maverick was a tall and slender man with dark short hair that looked freshly cut. It was an all business and no-nonsense kind of haircut. He was Winston's neighbor and they used to be friends when they were younger. Their friendship came to a halt when Winston became more and more involved with the family business and Maverick accused his friend of trying to put his own family out of business. Maverik became even more enraged when Winston started dating Sophie, clearly bothered by the fact that his old friend had time to date but not to mend their friendship. One day, Winston had caught Maverick trying to plant a kiss on Sophie's lips. They competed with one another ever since and Winston vowed to kill his former friend one day.

Maverick walked past Winston and out of the office without even a nod of the head, ignoring him completely.

"Mr. Hamilton, right on time." Principal Harper spoke.

Winston grabbed hold of the armrest and

wrenched his body up off the bench that only gave him a few fleeting moments of discomfort. He smiled at the perky and plump receptionist as he passed her desk and made his way into the principal's office. Once inside, he found a much more suitable chair waiting for him. The principal was dressed in a gray suit and had several patches of gray hair and a stern face, no doubt brought on by the town's most rebellious children. Even his beard was riddled with gray.

"So, what can I do for you, Mr. Hamilton?" the principal asked, closing the door and then taking a seat at his desk.

"I'll get straight to the point, as not to waste any of our time. You know the economy has been rough for all of Kosher Harbor since Hurricane Candi hit us. Even my family has suffered. I know times are…"

"Stop right there, Winston Hamilton." Principal Harper stood up out of his chair, his voice getting louder as he spoke. "If you think you're going to make an appointment to see me and come into my office just to tell me that you're raising the prices of the seafood for the fish fry this year, and with barely a full week's notice at that, you've got another thing coming! I can get the damn fish from someone else!"

Winston chuckled and shook his head. "Actually, what I was going to say before you interrupted me, was that I know times have been difficult since Hurricane Candi. I am willing to sponsor all of the seafood for the fish fry this year, completely free of charge."

Principal Harper snapped his mouth shut and sat back down. He straightened his tie and cleared his throat. He ran his fingers through his beard. "My sincerest apologies. I was out of line to assume the worst in you. You are very correct; Kosher Harbor has been suffering in silence. The school thanks you for your generosity."

"You are quite welcome."

"Honestly, that is quite the donation you will be making. Practically half of the town will be at the fish fry. Are you certain you want to feed everyone?"

"Yes, we are certain. Sophie is delighted and so is the rest of my family. Honestly, I will probably have to hire some helping hands outside my family. Which will also benefit their pockets. It's the least I can do. Kosher Harbor is my home. The people here are practically family to us. And I always make sure my family is well fed."

CHAPTER 5

It was still morning and the meeting with Principal Harper put Winston Hamilton in a good mood. A mood this good was rare for the elderly man, but nonetheless, he now had a bit of pep in his step as he made his way back to his car in the parking lot. He climbed into his vehicle and shut the door of his blue Buick Century with a snap. He threw the gear in reverse and started to back up before looking in his rearview mirror and then suddenly slammed on the brakes. Standing inches from his back bumper was Maverick Tucker, his old friend.

"You about hit me, you son-of-a-bitch!" Maverick yelled at him, slamming his fist into the truck of his car. The man was also elderly, so the hit did no damage to the car.

Winston got out of his car and laid into Maverick. "You touch my car again and I'll run you over right here, right now. What's the big idea of jumping behind my car when I'm trying to back up? You looking to get an insurance settlement? You've always been after my family's secrets, then you tried to steal Sophie away from me, and now you want our insurance money. Your father always was jealous of my father and you've always been jealous of me! I'm tired of your games, Maverick. I'll kill ya. I swear to God, I'll kill ya one day!"

"Oh, calm down. I wasn't trying to get hit, you old fool. I was trying to get your attention! Did Harper tell you about the cookoff?" Maverick asked.

"No. He didn't mention anything about a cookoff. Why?"

"Well, this year we're having a little competition between some of the seafood vendors. Who can cook the best dish. And guess what, I'm one of the judges!"

"You can't be a judge and have your wife enter the competition. You'll rig it!" Winston Hamilton proclaimed.

"Oh, you didn't hear the news? We're no longer in the seafood business. I got tired of competing with you, Winston. I done it for decades and since Hurricane Candi, the community's gotten tight with their money. This will be the last week we'll be selling seafood at the market."

Winston Hamilton smiled, baring all his teeth. It was a wicked smile, full of pride and evil. "I knew you'd give up sooner or later. You're a loser, Maverick! You never were a good businessman, let alone a fisherman."

"On the contrary, I'm an excellent businessman. I have realized that the market has too many fish vendors. I decided to not close shop, but to change shop. I'm going to start selling side dishes. Coleslaw, Cesar salad, pastas, fresh vegetables, mac and cheese, and of course potatoes of all kinds. My wife makes a killer scalloped potato dish. The town can buy your overpriced fish or choose from any other vendor to get their fish from. But what about the side dishes? I'll be the only one. That's why I volunteered to cater all the fixins for this year's fish fry, to spread the word to the entire town, all in one night."

Winston narrowed his eyes into a glare. The two old men had more in common than either of them wished to admit. "Well, I hope me putting you out of business won't count against my family's entries at the fish fry."

"I'm not out of business, you moron. I'm only *changing* the type of product I'm selling now."

"Sure. Sure," Winston said. "Whatever helps you sleep at night. Now move out of my way, or I really will run you down." Winston got back into his car and slammed the driver door shut. He flipped Maverick the middle finger as he passed him. Neither one of the men cared that a few of the school's teachers were watching the argument take place from a distance.

CHAPTER 6

Winston Hamilton pulled into the driveway of his luxurious property. No other family nor company owned as much land as the Hamilton's. The layout of Kosher Harbor is shaped like a jagged letter "M" and the Hamilton's property was located on the bottom right side.

The old man barged through the front door. "Sophie!" he yelled, not bothering to close the door behind him. "Sophie!" he yelled again, walking through the living room and entering the kitchen.

"What is it? What's wrong?" his wife asked. Her voice had a hint of worry in it.

"Good news! We put that damn fool Maverick Tucker out of business! He was just at the school and admitted to my face that he is gonna be selling salads and coleslaw instead of seafood."

"Why does that make you so happy? I don't see how it will change anything with what we do in the slightest," Sophie concluded.

"It changes everything! His little side dish stand won't last long and then he'll be broke. He'll be forced to sell his land. We can expand the family business! We could monopolize the entire seafood market and be the sole provider to feed all of Kosher Harbor, every damn day of the week!"

Winston and Sophie both turned their heads to the sound of the front door shutting. Footsteps could be heard coming closer and closer to the kitchen. "Who left the door open?" Evelyn asked as she entered the kitchen, her son Melvin following closely behind her. Evelyn's natural and brown curly hair bounced as she walked. She was dressed in jeans and a red blouse. And she stunk of handling fish all day from her earlier delivery. Her son Melvin was dressed in overhauls and had a permanent look of curiosity on his face. Unlike other kids his age, he did not possess a lot of energy. He didn't misbehave or annoy adults.

"And another thing," Winston continued, ignoring Evelyn's question. "I decided that we are going to sponsor all of the seafood for the fish fry next week, free of charge."

Evelyn gasped. Sophie clutched her pearl necklace and almost fell over her own feet. "Why?" they both asked at the same time.

"Winston, we will be losing out on a great bit of money if we do this for nothing." Sophie said.

"It's not for nothing. There are people in this town who hate us, I remind you. And there are people who cannot afford to buy our seafood delights. Think of this as giving them a free sample of our secret recipe. If they love it, they'll come back for more with their wallets. Also, practically half the town will be at the school. And, while they're all stuffing their faces, Evelyn can run a few errands for me, unnoticed... I would like some dirt on Maverick."

Evelyn looked down at Melvin. "Go outside and play now. But don't go too far. Stay where I can see you and don't go near the water. Or the barn again either." The little boy nodded his head and did as his mother told him.

Close to the property's edge stood a large brown barn that used to be painted vibrant red. The years of weather and neglect had aged the wood. It did not hold cattle like most farm barns did. Its doors were chained and locked. Evelyn hated looking at it. She knew what was inside and it disgusted her. The Hamilton secret was locked inside that barn. A secret that would destroy all of Kosher Harbor if it got out to the public. No one could know the family secret. Evelyn wished she could forget.

"What kind of dirt do you need on Maverick?" Evelyn asked her father-in-law, coming back to her senses.

"We'll discuss it later. Right now, we need bait."

Evelyn nodded and then left the kitchen.

"At the fish fry, they're doing a cookoff. Sophie, Maverick is one of the judges. I'll need you to cook up a prize-winning dish for him. One that he'll never forget…"

"I can handle that. But what about the rest of the town? Who's going to cook for them? Did you give it any thought before you volunteered to be Santa Clause?"

Winston scoffed. He had thought of that already. He knew the rest of the family would be too busy and he knew they would need another hand to help feed most the community. "I already thought that through. I'm sure someone in this town needs some extra money and would be willing to give a helping hand."

Sophie smirked. "Now that you mention it, I have the perfect person in mind for the job."

Evelyn entered back into the kitchen holding her son Melvin by the hand. Her face was white and her curly hair looked wild. In her other hand she was holding bolt cutters with red handles. "Someone broke into the barn!" she blurted the words out.

Melvin's eyes were wide and full of fear. "I saw the door open and when I got closer, a man ran out and knocked me down," he said with a shaky voice. Tears started to form in his eyes.

Three things happened simultaneously. First, the phone started to ring. Second, someone knocked on the front door, the sound echoing throughout the house. And last, Sophie gasped and clutched her hand around her pearl necklace with a shaking hand.

CHAPTER 7

Winston put his finger up to his lips, telling everyone to be quiet. No one spoke. No one moved. Even Melvin knew something serious was happening and it scared the boy. He was anxious. He was always told to stay away from the barn but no one ever told him why. He was too afraid to ask about what he saw inside, although his curiosity was almost too much to handle. He decided to keep his mouth shut.

"Sophie, see who is at the door. Whatever you do, do not let them into the house. Not without a warrant from a judge. Even if they have one, I'm sure we can buy our way out of it. Evelyn, take Melvin to his room and stay there until I call for you." Winston spoke with authority but he was unshaken by the continuous knocking at the front door and the phone ringing off the hook.

"Winston, Melvin said there was a man who came out of the barn. This will ruin us!"

"We will discuss it later! Now, do as I tell you. Sophie, answer the goddamn door!"

Evelyn looked down at Melvin. "Come on, let's go play. Everything will be alright." She led her son down the hall and up the stairs out of sight. She wanted to reassure her son that he wasn't in trouble but that might be a lie. He indeed might be in extreme trouble. Evelyn wondered if Melvin went inside the barn. She must have told him a dozen times to stay away from it. Why would he even go *near* the damn thing?

Sophie straightened her clothes and ran her fingers through her blonde hair and followed behind them to see who was at the front door.

Winston pushed the TALK button on the cordless home phone and placed it up to his ear. "Winston speaking. What can I do for you?"

"Winston! Sorry to bother you, I know you're a busy man. I forgot to tell you earlier…"

"Who the hell is this?" Winston interrupted the

man on the other line.

"Erm… Sorry. This is Principal Harper," he stammered. "I got your number from Melvin's emergency contact information in his file.

"Oh, what can I do for you?" Winston's voice changed back to a more respectful tone.

"I forgot to tell you. We're doing a cookoff at the fish fry. There will be three judges: Dr. David Hanus, Maverick Tucker, and myself. Do you want to sign up to compete? A few of the other seafood vendors are entering."

Yes, that sounds grand. Sign Sophie and myself up. And Evelyn, our daughter-in-law. We'll see you Friday. Thanks for calling."

"Can't wait. Thanks again, Winston."

Winston pressed the END button to end the call. He walked out of the kitchen to see who Sophie was talking to. Just as he entered the living room, Sophie was shutting the front door.

"Who was that?" Winston asked.

Sophie peered out the window for a moment before answering. "It was Dr. Hanus. He was dropping off our Propofol prescription."

"Propofol? We just had it refilled last week. He's never done house calls like this before," Winston said.

"I know," Sophie replied. "And his shoes were muddy too. Why would his shoes be muddy? Is there mud by the barn? Who was on the phone?"

"Principal Harper. Wanted to tell me about a competition with the judges at the fish fry. He seemed nervous though. And he got our number from snooping through Melvin's school files. Seems a bit fishy to me too." Winston clenched his fist together. Someone was trespassing and prying on his property and in his family business. He needed to find out who and what they knew. And then he needed to kill them.

"Evelyn!" Winston yelled.

Evelyn came back down stairs and was about to speak but was cut off.

"Who was this man you saw at the barn? Tell me, did you recognize him? Was it one of our neighbors?"

"I'm not sure. I didn't actually see anyone. I only saw Melvin standing close to the barn. He told me a man came running out of the barn and that he ran behind it. I asked him what he looked like but his description was vague. Only that he was wearing a mask and a black sweater. Who walks around dressed in all black in broad daylight? But he left his bolt cutter lying next to the barn doors. Or are they yours?" Evelyn pointed to where she dropped the tool moments ago next to the back kitchen door.

Winston looked at the tool but he did not recognize it as his own. "I've never saw these before. But that's not much to go on. These bolt cutters could belong to anyone within Kosher Harbor. What color shirt was Dr. Hanus wearing, Sophie?"

"Blue. It was a blue button down. But his shoes were caked in mud. He could have easily pulled the sweater and mask off before coming to our door."

Winston pondered for a moment. "Sophie, you'll come with me. We're going to the hardware store for a new lock. Evelyn, when we get back have the kitchen prepped. We will need to start cooking for the fish fry. If the bolt cutters were on the outside of the barn, then there's a good chance that the intruder did not see anything to worry about."

"Can I go back to my room and play?" Melvin asked his mom.

"Yes, sweetie. But you need to stay away from the

barn. I've told you a dozen times now. That man could have hurt you," Evelyn said. She was deeply worried about her son's wellbeing and safety. She was the only one that was.

CHAPTER 8

Melvin darted up the stairs to his bedroom. He slammed his door shut, ran to the window and peered out. His view overlooked the back of the property, which included the brown barn. His view also included a small white tool shed that belonged to the Tucker's, and a small intersection that led to the main road which his grandparents always took when they left. Melvin looked from the barn to the stop sign. He looked back and forth between the two, impatiently waiting.

Finally, his grandfather's blue Buick pulled up to the stop sign and turned, without completely stopping. Melvin looked back to the barn and watched. Another moment passed before he spotted his mother making her way down to the barn.

Melvin dashed back out of his room and down the stairs. He ran down the hall and into the kitchen, almost slipping on the black and white marbled tiles that made up the kitchen floor. Melvin quickly grabbed the bolt cutters he had stolen from the Tucker's shed the previous week. The boy took the bolt cutters back upstairs with him to his bedroom.

Melvin went to his window again and stared at the brown barn; the same barn he was forbidden to go near, let alone inside of. But that's what made it all the more exciting for him. His mother always warned him about the barn but never explained the dangers of what laid within its walls. What was more curious, was that his grandparents never mentioned the barn to him; as if they didn't care if he went inside or not. His curiosity got the best of him. If his grandparents didn't warn him, then why was his mother always nagging him about playing safe and keeping away from the barn every time he went outside.

Melvin had enough of the secrets they kept from him. The boy thought it over one night and decided to act on those thoughts. He started out by getting close to the barn one day. The next, he dared himself to touch the side of the barn. And the day after, he touched the doors. That's the day he noticed the padlock. That's the day his interest really spiked. What were they keeping locked inside that was so dangerous?

Melvin thought about it again and again. He needed a way into the barn. He needed to steal the key! Days and nights searching for the correct key (when he was left alone) was unsuccessful. Any sets of keys that were left lying around were either a car key, front door key, or it did not fit the lock. Melvin grew tired of keys, and one night while watching his grandmother chop up a fish for dinner, he got the idea to chop the lock off. All he needed was the right tool, and he knew just where to get one.

Evelyn came out of the barn carrying multiple five-gallon stainless steel buckets. Melvin had no idea what the buckets were used for. This wasn't the first time he watched his mom carry them into the kitchen. He was always told to go up to his room and not to come out until they called for him.

Melvin left his room again and listened. He could hear his mom moving items around down in the kitchen.

He knew she was preparing the kitchen. He watched them filet fish before but only once. Melvin didn't like the smell of fish nor did he like the taste. It made him gag and he refused to ever try it again. Like most children, he was a fickle eater.

With the bolt cutters in hand, Melvin entered the guest bathroom and quietly shut the door behind him. He opened the bathroom's only window and chucked the cutters out and to the ground below. Melvin then climbed outside the window, holding onto the metal antenna tower that was attached to the house. Melvin shut the window and then began his descend down. The boy wasn't afraid of heights. He made this trip several times before. Once on the ground, he grabbed the cutters and ran to the brown barn at the property's edge. He knew his mom would be too busy to notice him.

The barn doors were shut, but not locked. Melvin slipped inside, leaving the door cracked open to illuminate the dark. The boy raked his eyes over his surroundings for the second time today. The barn was mostly empty. Any noise he made echoed off the walls. Stacked up next to the side of the doors were more of the galvanized metal buckets of various shapes and sizes. On the other side were your typical yard tools: rakes, shovels, garden forks, and loppers.

Where stables should have been was a large industrial freezer. It was like the one the cafeteria had at his school, but much, much bigger. He remembered the previous year when his grandfather had it installed. The digital thermometer was lit up with green numbers and read 29 degrees. Its door was locked with a padlock.

Melvin's curiosity was stronger than his fear. It was probably filled with fish. He hated fish. It would probably stink. He started toward the freezer with the bolt cutters in hand. He reached the door and put the tool up to the lock. He didn't struggle to break this lock like he did the first time earlier today. This time he held the tool by the ends of its handle and squeezed them together. The lock broke and he let it drop to the floor with a clang.

Melvin froze. He heard something coming from below his feet, through the floorboards. It sounded like yelling. He couldn't distinguish the noises. He continued to listen and the loud noises from under him slowly faded out again. Mumbles and murmurs could still be heard, but he couldn't understand anything that was being said.

He turned his attention and curiosity back to the freezer. Melvin grabbed hold of the door's handle and pulled. It took him a few good tugs to get it open. A curtain of thick plastic flaps hanged on the other side of the door and nothing but darkness laid behind them. Melvin pushed the button under the green digital numbers that had a lightbulb symbol on it. A light on the other side of the plastic flaps clicked on. He tried making out what was on the inside but the flaps were covered in frost and he couldn't make anything out.

The little boy reached his hand out in front of him and pushed it through the plastic flaps. He held it there for a moment, anticipating that something would grab him on the other side and yank him through.

Nothing happened. Melvin placed his other hand through and parted the flaps. A wave a freezing air rushed out and into his face. It sent shivers down his spine and his body convulsed from the sudden change in temperature.

He stepped inside the freezer and glanced around. Hanging from oversized, rusted hooks were large slabs of meat. They were inside clear plastic bags and also covered in frost. There had to be close to one hundred slabs of meat, most of which were bigger than his own body, hanging from the ceiling of the freezer.

Melvin got closer to one to inspect it. He reached as high as his fingers could and wiped off the frost from the plastic. It took him a moment to realize what he was looking at. Under the plastic wasn't frozen fish or just a slab of meat. He was looking at the naked body of a man. The hook the body was hanging from protruded from the man's chest. What little blood was around the wound was frozen. The skin had a light blue tint to it.

Melvin went to the next hanging body and wiped the frost away from the plastic that covered it. This time it was a woman's naked body. He went to the next, and the next. He used his hand to wipe frost away from all the plastic to see their naked, dead bodies. The child was observing the body of one of the hanging men. The large hook was poking out just under his ribs, in the center of his chest. He made a mental note of the size of his areolas. This man has muscular arms and a flat stomach. And hairs under his bellybutton that led down…

Without warning, the freezer door shut. It was fast and hard. Someone slammed it shut on purpose, locking him inside. The noise made Melvin jump with a start. He looked to the door but did not move. Then the lights above his head went off. The child stood in complete darkness with at least one hundred frozen, hanging bodies all around him.

CHAPTER 9

Melvin did not move. He did not scream for help or start to cry. He stood in the cold and in the dark, waiting. He was not afraid of the dead bodies that he was trapped with. He was not afraid of freezing to death. He felt nothing in that moment. In fact, it had been a long time since he felt anything at all...

After a few minutes, the lights came back on and the door opened. "Get out here," Grandpa Winston said from the other side of the plastic flaps.

Melvin did as he was told and walked out of the freezer. His grandpa was holding the padlock he had cut off but did not seem upset that he was in the freezer, inside the barn that he was not supposed to go near.

"What do you have to say for yourself?" his grandpa asked him.

Melvin shrugged. "I was curious."

"There was no man who broke in here, was there? It was you all along. You made up that story of a man being in here, didn't you?"

Melvin nodded. "I didn't want to get in trouble."

"Don't ever lie to me," Winston said to his grandson. He placed his hands on his shoulders. "What do you think about what you saw in there?"

Melvin thought for a moment before answering. "I think it's neat. I never saw a dead body before. But why are they in there?" the boy asked.

"You're a little young. But there's no point of waiting to break you in now. They're hookbait. Unclaimed bodies from the destruction leftover by Hurricane Candi. We found them and we're going to use them to feed the fish we catch to make them bigger. It's the family business. It's also a family secret. No one else can ever know."

Melvin nodded his head again, indicating that he understood. Then he heard it again; mumbling from below his feet. "What's that?" he asked, pointing to the floorboards they stood on.

"They're hookbait too. Distant relatives who weren't born first, like we were," Winston said. "They're born and raised as fish bait. We're different, you and I. We're firstborn sons in the Hamilton bloodline. We're special. It's alright to feel different than other people. They don't understand us. They're not special like we are. Now come on, let's go back inside. And don't tell your mother you were in here."

Melvin followed his grandpa out of the barn and he locked the door with a new padlock. They entered the kitchen through the back door and found Evelyn laying out various knives on one of the countertops. The galvanized buckets were placed on the floor beside her.

"I replaced all the barn locks with these industrial ones, just in case. Here is one of the keys," Winston said to Evelyn.

She took the key and slipped it into her pocket. "I thought you were upstairs in your room playing," she said to Melvin.

Melvin felt his grandfather's eyes on the back of his head. "I got bored so I went outside."

"Well, it's time for you to go to your room and

stay there this time until we call you back down," Evelyn ordered her son.

Melvin looked back to his grandpa and gave the old man a smile before leaving the kitchen and going back to his room. He was grateful that he didn't tell his mom on him.

"What are we going to do about the strange man who Melvin saw earlier?" Evelyn asked Winston.

"It will be delt with whenever we find out who it was. Now, go get some fresh hookbait."

Evelyn left the kitchen and went to the barn. When she returned through the screen door, she wasn't alone. A tall man was with her. He was pale as an eggshell and skinny; malnourished his entire life. He wore no shoes or clothes whatsoever. "Climb up on the butcher block and lay back. Then you can go to sleep," Evelyn said to the man. "I gave him some Propofol, but it hasn't fully kicked in yet."

The mysterious man laid down on the butcher countertop and looked at Evelyn, waiting.

Winston pulled up his shirt sleeves and grabbed a hatchet that was hanging on the kitchen wall. Its blade was nine inches wide and despite its age, was very sharp.

"We don't have time for that. We're on a deadline," he scowled. With one swift movement, he raised the sharp weapon above his head and slammed it down into the man's neck. The head detached from the body and hit the floor with a thud. Blood splattered across the kitchen as it spewed out from both the carotid arteries, now fully exposed.

Winston continued chopping his relative's limbs from his torso. This was not the first time Winston had chopped up another human into pieces, and he knew that it wouldn't be the last. There were no negative emotions in his eyes as he cut up his own flesh and blood with perfect precision. Instead, he felt an anticipation, knowing the fish were going to thrive on these nutrients, and worked skillfully. The body on his butcher block was nobody he once loved. He didn't even see him as a human; it was hookbait, and nothing more.

For generations, the Hamilton family had always favored the firstborn son. Any other children that were born were sent to the barn. They were nothing more than fish cattle. They were nothing more than a squirming worm on a hook. And that is exactly what the Hamilton's used them for. Winston did not know when his family first used a human to lure the fish. All he knew was that it worked. As the favored firstborn son himself, he was taught to see others beneath him, not as people. They were not people. They were vermin. They were slabs of meat.

The Hamilton's used the flesh and blood of their own family members to draw the fish in. The fish would gobble the meat up and grow bigger and bigger. The fish around the Hamilton property would breed bigger fish with their superior DNA from being fed human flesh for generations after generations. It was Sophie's idea to grind the leftover bones up into a powder. The same powder she gave to Jillian. It was full of protein and it was easier to get rid of the evidence as well. Once a fish was big enough, the Hamilton's would remove it from the water to sell at their local seafood market. No other stand had fish quite as big and juicy as the Hamilton's catch. It was the family recipe; the family's *secret* recipe for success.

"Sophie, come get this. It's ready," ordered Winston, using a squeegee to scrape blood and bits of human gristle from the table into a galvanized bucket below. Even those bits would be saved and spread into the waters for the fish to feast upon. The blood they collected was saved, and then periodically put into the water to attract the more aggressive fish. The Hamilton's tried to waste very little of their bait.

Sophie reached around Winston and grabbed the severed limbs laying on the counter. She walked across the kitchen, limbs in tow, and placed them on another counter. She grabbed a seven-inch filleting knife and began sharpening it.

The innocent teenage girl that Winston fell in love with was long gone. Sophie could put on a charming show when she needed to. Her caring and thoughtful instructions on suggestions of how to prepare the fish made their customers trust their family, and the townsfolk often asked her for the secret to their successful fish yields. She'd smile and say she couldn't reveal such things, only that her husband was just a skilled fisherman. But Sophie knew. Winston had trained her well throughout the years, both with preparing hookbait and even private acting lessons. The woman she became was now nothing more than a two faced conniving evil snake.

"I love this new knife you bought for me. The meat comes off the bone so easily. It's like cutting through warm butter." Sophie took pride in her work now, enjoying the feel of her knife cutting through the flesh ever so smoothly. She'd practiced for years and felt she had honed her craft to perfection. She could cut through fat and muscle just as precisely as a surgeon.

"I'm glad you like it. I figured you had enough jewelry, and a new filleting knife would be a suitable anniversary gift," Winston replied, scratching an itch on his face. The blood from his hands smeared onto the side of his nose, but he didn't care. Each time she sliced through the skin, both of them heard a soft tearing sound that was like music to their ears. They'd dance to it if anyone else knew how to replicate such a perfect sound. He smiled lovingly at his wife, looking into her eyes, and she smiled back.

This was their quality time. They were often busy with their work, and it was nice to have some time together, doing what they loved. Winston appreciated the finer things in life, and Sophie was one of those things. He was so proud of the woman she had become. He watched her skillfully remove the femoral artery from the severed thigh, impressed how she managed to keep it fully intact, and fell even more in love with her.

Sophie continued carving the flesh from the bone. She tossed the meat into the five-gallon bucket beside Winston's table, and chunked the flesh into another at her own feet. Once the femur, fibula, and tibia were stripped down to bare bloody bones, Sophie gave them back to Winston. She would handle the meaty bits and her beloved husband would tend to grinding the bones down.

"Evelyn!" Sophie yelled at her. "Bring more bait. We're going to need more. Hurry up!" She ordered. Her husband was standing there watching her. As much as she adored the attention she was receiving, Winston needed to be working. They were on a deadline. The fish fry was just around the corner and they wanted to impress the town with the fattest, heartiest fish possible.

Evelyn nodded and ran out of the kitchen through the back door, the screen door slamming shut behind her. It was only a few minutes later when she returned with another distant relative from the ominous barn.

The Hamilton's kept the relatives in line by brainwashing; telling them since birth that they were to serve a higher purpose. They had to be kept out of public sight at all times, otherwise when their beauty was seen, the public would try to take them away. It was a lie that worked for decades. In fact, the Hamilton relatives were not beautiful at all. They were disfigured and misshapen, a consequence of trying to keep the bloodline as pure as possible and the secret kept quiet.

The distant relatives that they cared for and pretended to love needed that false security to keep them docile. Evelyn felt no guilt over her deception nor any sadness bringing her in-law relatives to the chopping block. After all these years, she was used to the chore and tried not to think of them as people. When she did, she felt sad for her son more than the ones who were locked away in the barn. The man she guided into the kitchen was actually grinning. The excitement of finally being chosen was apparent on his face.

Winston took the man from Evelyn. "Thank you for your sacrifice," he said before slicing his throat open. The man gasped his last breath as his blood flowed down his neck and torso. It dripped onto Winston's arms as he continued to hold one of his relatives upright. The blood splashed on his shoes, and soaked through his dress shirt when the man fell into him, unable to remain on his feet.

The kitchen was a bloody mess, as well was Winston. That didn't concern him though. Sophie came over to help Winston lift the limp man onto the counter top. Blood saturated her clothes as well, and they both tried to remain quiet enough to hear the death rattle in the vermin's throat. The Hamilton's enjoyed the sounds of death; the squelches of blood, the last few raspy breaths, and then the silence that followed.

The bait's eyes had grown dull and lifeless. Evelyn ran her fingers over his hair, smoothing it down. "There, there. You've done well for your family. We're proud of you," she said, and closed his eyes. She knew Winston didn't care if the eyes were open or shut when he removed the head, but it felt symbolic to close them.

Winston began getting to work on the fresh body. Once again, he used his hatchet to remove the head first. The severed head thudded as it hit the ground by his feet, briefly impeding his work. He kicked it aside in irritation. Winston's movements were a delicate dance while he worked drawing and quartering the body, and he couldn't be disturbed by a head rolling around.

Sophie picked it up by the hair and placed it on the countertop and began her work. The brains of the degenerate hookbait provided no growth to the fish, and served as just a treat. They especially seemed to love the eyes and the lips. It was probably the texture they enjoyed. They were the appetizer for the fish, as caviar is an appetizer for humans.

The Hamilton's continued chopping, slicing, and breaking down the bodies of their family members, one after another, for several hours. They worked meticulously as Winston demanded nothing but perfection. Between fetching more bodies, and replacing buckets, Evelyn would stay at attention, watching Winston and Sophie work, learning and observing their techniques.

"Evelyn, we need more bait. Bring more bodies!" Winston yelled.

"Should I use the *other* bodies? We already used the last adult in your bloodline. There are only a few fresh children left. We can't use the children, can we?" Evelyn asked, looking at the heads of their victims that lay scattered around the floor by Sophie's feet. She counted seven.

Although she knew the children were little more than wild animals, she was horrified by the idea of using them. They were young, like her son. Their bodies weren't grown yet, and they didn't have enough blood or muscle. They probably needed four or five more adult bodies, but if using children, they'd need to use at least eight to ten. Besides, the thought of children seemed…wrong. They needed to grow up first. Killing most of the children before they had grown would severely limit the future breeding cycle more than they already had.

Winston and Sophie both glared at her with disdain and anger for questioning them.

"I said, bring me more bait! Now!" Winston roared at his daughter-in-law. Spit flew from his lips as he screamed at her. He didn't like to be questioned, and he certainly didn't like to be disobeyed. His wild eyes flashed murder at Evelyn, and he raised the hatchet he held in his hand, shaking it at her. "Go! Now!"

Evelyn's mouth dried and her body started trembling. She had the feeling that if she didn't do as he said this second, he'd consider putting her on the chopping block. She quickly turned away from her bloodied father-in-law and rushed to the barn. She would bring the last few children to them first. And if they still demanded more bodies, she would unlock and enter the freezer for the first time.

CHAPTER 10

It was early, Friday morning. The day before the fish fry. Winston and Sophie both woke up, delighted. The memory of dismembering body, after body, after body, was still fresh in their minds and they both were still basking in the high it gave them.

The fish had gone wild the previous night when the happy couple chunked the flesh of chopped up meat and organs of their distant relatives into the water off their many piers that was on their property. Winston and Sophie stood on Pier twenty-nine, located on the corner of their property, close to the brown barn. They held hands, watching the sun set, as the fish splashed wildly, trying to eat as much as their bellies could hold. Once the water had calmed down a bit, the Hamilton's pulled their nets in. The fish captured was plenty enough to feed the town, and then some.

Sophie called for Evelyn to take her place with Winston to finish hand picking, and killing the last fish. It was now closer to midnight than not, but Sophie didn't care. The fish fry was the next day and they still needed to hire someone to help them cook. Sophie started her car and took her time, driving slowly along the coast line of the harbor, enjoying the view, as she made her way to the house on Pier Seventeen.

Once she had arrived at the brightly green painted house, she unlatched the white gate and walked up the steps to the front door. She rang the doorbell and waited a few seconds, and then rang it again. She knew the household was asleep but that wasn't important. She rang the bell once again.

A few seconds later, she heard a voice call out. "Who is it?" Mitchel Parker said on the other side of the door."

"Sophie Hamilton," she answered. "I need to speak with Jillian."

Mitchel answered the door, "Sophie? It's after midnight."

"Yes, I am fully aware of the time, Mitch. Can you wake Jillian. It's important."

Mitchel gave the woman an odd look. He opened the door wider and invited the older woman inside. He left her alone, and made his way back upstairs to get his wife.

"Sophie? Is everything alright?" Jillian asked, making her way down the stairs with her husband following behind her.

"Oh, Jillian!" Sophie's voice was much more frantic now as she spewed lies from her lips. "I need your help! The school contacted us last minute about the fish fry. They needed us to help feed everyone tomorrow morning. Evelyn said it was a great idea and that she would help but she has fallen ill. Now I'm in over my head. Can you please be a friend, and help us?"

Jillian was quiet, unsure of what to say, and still half asleep. Mitchel was more alert, and annoyed. "And you waited until midnight to ask?"

"I do apologize for such the late intrusion. Evelyn had just started to get sick and I became so overwhelmed. I started to have a panic attack and then Winston tried to calm me down but it just started an argument between us.

Now he isn't speaking to me and I got angry and just left. I'm really in a bind. I could really use your help. I know you're a great cook. You told me so when you told me you were pregnant the other day."

Jillian's eyes widened in disbelief. How could Sophie do this to her?

"You're pregnant?" Mitchel asked, shocked to hear the news for the first time.

Jillian looked to her husband and then to Sophie. She looked back at her husband. "Mitchel, I'm sorry. I was going to tell you earlier, but I was afraid."

"Afraid? Of what? Why would you be afraid to tell me that I'm going to be a father? What are you afraid of, Jillian?" he asked, his voice getting louder with each word.

"I'm afraid of everything!" Jillian yelled back. "What if I'm no good at being a mother?"

"I'm sorry, to the both of you. I thought she had told you. She did plan on telling you. She told me herself she was going to tell you the day she bought the trout from me. Please don't be upset with Jillian. But it is awfully late. Will you be able to help me, Jillian?" Sophie asked again, changing the subject back to her.

"Yes, of course I'll help."

"Fantastic!" Sophie yelled; her entire fake mood shifted. She grabbed Jillian's hand and started to pull her out the door, not caring that she was still in her pajamas and barefoot.

CHAPTER 11

Sophie pushed the gas pedal to the floor and was speeding down the highway within minutes after leaving the Parker's home. Jillian held on tight, her body jerking from side to side as Sophie rounded the curves at an accelerated speed. Her driving reminded Jillian of Cruella de Vil.

"Sophie, slow down! You're driving way too fast."

Sophie glared at Jillian for a split second, before softening her expression. "I'm sorry, my dear. But you insisted on talking to Mitch and changing your clothes. We lost so much time because of your inability to tell him about this child that you're carrying inside of you. Why were you so ashamed to tell him you were pregnant? It is his child, isn't it?"

"I wasn't ashamed," Jillian said. "I had planned on telling *Mitchel*." She emphasized her husband's name as to correct Sophie from calling him anything other than that. "But when he returned home from work, he wasn't in a pleasant mood. I decided to wait for this weekend instead. And of course, the baby is his!"

Sophie took another curve on the bank of the harbor as she still sped down the highway. The tires squealed as the car fishtailed for a moment before straightening itself. "Well, I wish you would have phoned me and told me before I made a fool of myself by letting that little detail slip. I do not like drama, Jillian. Honestly, I thought we were friends."

Jillian stared at Sophie in the dark car. She was too tired to argue. She was too tired to think. What was she doing at this time of night in a car with a woman she hardly knew? Jillian ignored her new *friend* and stared out the passenger window for the rest of the car ride in silence.

"Would you like a cup of hot tea?" Sophie asked Jillian as they made their way into the Hamilton mansion.

"Perhaps a hot cup of coffee? I'm still half

asleep," Jillian replied, and then let out a long yawn as she covered her mouth with the back of her hand.

Sophie made her way directly to the kitchen. As they entered, Jillian looked around. The kitchen was spotless. Nothing was out of place and there was an abundance of counter space with a large butcher block island in the center of the kitchen. The wood itself looked as if it had just been freshly stained with a glossy chocolate color. A vase of roses rested in its center, bringing some color into the room.

"Have a seat while I brew us some java," Sophie spoke as she busied herself in the corner of the kitchen with her back turned to Jillian. "We can discuss the plans while we sip. That will leave us with prepping for the fish fry, which should only take us four to five hours. Then we can sleep for a couple hours before we travel to the school."

Jillian stared in disbelief. How could she expect a pregnant woman to work throughout the night with hardly any sleep and then expect her to work again during the day!

"Do you wish for cream or sugar?" Sophie asked.
"Yes, please. Both."

Sophie reached into a cabinet and brought down two different sized jars, both filled with a white substance. Jillian wasn't paying attention to her. Instead, she was patting her pockets, looking for her cell phone. She must have forgotten it at home. She let out a sigh. She wanted to text Mitchel to check on him. Sophie was rushing her out the door and hardly gave the couple two minutes to talk about the baby. She just wanted everything between them to work out. Jillian hoped that Mitchel wasn't upset with her.

"Here you go. Be careful, it's hot," Sophie said as she slid the steaming cup over to Jillian. She secretly watched Jillian take a sip of the hot coffee. Sophie's smile widened as Jillian swallowed the beverage.

"How does it taste?" Sophie asked her friend.

"It's good. Thank you. It's just what I needed."

Sophie smiled again; this time all her teeth were showing. It was a smile of a shark that was ready to attack at any given moment as it stalked its prey, circling underneath them. Sophie took a sip from her own cup and swallowed.

The two women sat side by side with a pad of paper between them. Jillian wrote as Sophie spoke. They planned out three menus: the first for the judges, the second for the adults, and the third for the children of Kosher Harbor. Sophie seemed tickled at the thought of feeding the entire town their fish; especially the children. They would love deep fried fish sticks.

CHAPTER 12

Sophie and Jillian worked throughout the night as the morning of the town's annual fish fry crept up on them. Sophie bossed Jillian around in the kitchen, correcting her how to hold the knife and where to cut the fish. Sophie insisted the portion sizes were inconsistent and the longer the night went on, the more Jillian wished Mitchel had never answered the door.

"Good morning, ladies," Winston greeted the two in the kitchen as he entered. He gave Sophie a quick peck on the lips. "Did either of you get any sleep?"

"Not a wink," Sophie answered. "I thought Jillian was up for the job, but I think a fish fry was out of her league."

Jillian stopped what she was doing, clearly

agitated with her so-called friend. "Is that any way to speak to the one person who bailed you out last night?" Jillian pointed to the various coolers that were filled with different types of fish in them, each cut to portion size. "Without me, not even half of those coolers would have been filled. You barely lifted a damn finger, Sophie!"

Sophie exhaled a sigh of horror. She grabbed the strand of pearls that hung from her neck, but did not speak a word. Her hand started to tremble.

Winston took a step toward Jillian. "Now listen here, Mrs. Parker, you are not to talk to my wife that way. And in *our* own home. I think it best for you to leave now."

"Yes, I think that best too," Sophie added. "I brewed fresh coffee for you, at your request, at one in the morning. That's what friends do. They help one another out. And you being with child, shouldn't even be drinking coffee. But do you even think of your baby? No. It seems that Jillian only thinks of herself! Now, please leave our home."

Surprised at the turn of events, Jillian laughed out loud. The Hamilton's stared her down in all seriousness. Jillian felt used and even a bit abused by the couple. She excused herself from the kitchen and left their home. Once outside, she remembered that she was brought here by Sophie and did not have a way back to her own home. She didn't even have her cell phone on her. Jillian shook her head in disbelief as she started to walk down their long driveway, away from the oversized white house.

Back inside the kitchen, Sophie and Winston were locked together at the lips. The twisted couple enjoyed when others suffered. It was a turn on for them both.

"Good morning," Evelyn interrupted as she came into the kitchen. Evelyn was already showered and dressed for the day. She did not look sick in the slightest. Sophie had lied about that too. "I heard Jillian leave, so I thought I'd come down to finish helping."

Together, Winston, Sophie, and Evelyn, loaded the coolers of raw fish in the car's trunk. Evelyn buckled her son, Melvin, in the backseat and kissed him on the forehead. "Be good for grandpa and grandma. I'll see you later tonight."

"You're not coming, mommy?" the boy pleaded, looking up at Evelyn.

Letting her son go without her was hard for Evelyn. But there was no way around it. Evelyn had errands to run for her in-laws. She also had her own errands to run. She knew Melvin was growing up too fast and she knew she had to prepare for their escape from her wicked family. The thought of the strange man dressed in black barging out of the barn with her son right by the doors still frightened her. She had to get him away from this place. She ruffled the boy's thick hair. "I promise, I'll see you after the fish fry. Even if I did come with you, you would be too busy playing with your friends. You won't even have time to miss me. Now be a good little boy and mind grandpa and grandma."

Evelyn shut the car door and watched as her son and her in-laws drove away. The fish fry would start in a couple hours. She would use that time to do her own errands first. Once the fish fry was ongoing, she would do what her grandfather asked of her, and be back home before it was over. The most important thing was that no one was to see her. Her alibi depended on it.

It wasn't long before the Hamilton's were a couple miles down the road before spotting Jillian. She was walking on the side of the road, looking frail.

"Winston, pull over. I am a bit famished after not sleeping. I really could use the help of Jillian today. Do you mind if we pay her? It will be the only way she will get in the car."

Winston passed Jillian and pulled onto the side of the road.

"Jillian," Sophie yelled her name out the passenger window. "Oh, Jillian. I just feel awful how we left things this morning. I guess it's the lack of sleep that got to us both. Friends do have fights sometimes after all."

Jillian stopped in her tracks. "I am not your friend, Sophie. Now leave me alone. I want nothing to do with you anymore."

Sophie unbuckled her seatbelt and opened her door. "Please, don't be mad. I was very tired and wasn't thinking correctly earlier. Please, get in the car. I really do still need your help today," she pleaded.

"Absolutely not! You made a fool of me this morning. And I worked hard for you. And for what? Nothing. Now, I'm tired, I'm pregnant, and I just want to get home to Mitchel. Just leave me alone."

"Mitchel thinks that you'll be at the fish fry. He won't even be home by time you get there. Please, get in the car. I hate to see you walking like this while you're pregnant."

"You should have thought about that before you and your husband kicked me out of your house," Jillian snapped back.

"He apologizes. We both do. And here, we still plan on paying you for all your work and troubles." Sophie reached into her purple and black polka dotted clutch and pulled out several hundred-dollar bills.

"I don't want your money," Jillian proclaimed.

"Don't be foolish. Everyone in Kosher Harbor wants our money. Now, think of the baby. The baby will have needs. Use this money for the baby. What were you going to name her? Little Sandy Parker?" Sophie reached back into her clutch and pulled out several more hundreds. "Here is one thousand dollars. You can start a college fund for the little tyke."

Jillian looked at the money and hesitated. A thousand dollars for one long day was a lot of money. They had been struggling since Hurricane Candi hit last year. They had only lived in their house for a month before the storm damaged it. Insurance didn't cover everything they lost. They could use the money.

"It's all I have right now, but I promise you I'll

throw in an extra thousand after the fish fry is over."

Jillian was going to ask for another apology but once Sophie offered another thousand, she realized she rather have the money than an insincere apology. She smiled at the older woman and nodded before opening the backseat door and climbing in. She clicked the seatbelt and smiled at the little boy sitting next to her.

CHAPTER 13

The Hamilton's, along with Jillian, pulled into a parking spot at the school's back parking lot. Principal Harper was already walking to their car to help them before Winston had the chance to cut the engine off.

"Right on time, right on time!" Principal Harper said, extending his hand to shake Winston's as he exited the car.

"It's swell to see you again, Harper. Where do we set up? We got all the fish in coolers."

Sophie cleared her throat.

"My apologies, you remember my wife, Sophie? And you already know our grandson, Melvin. He's going to inherit the Hamilton fortune one day, as long as he minds his manners and continues to do well in school."

Principal Harper nodded his head at Sophie and shook the child's hand. "Quite the handshake you got there, Melvin. It's good to see you again."

"Thank you," Melvin responded.

Principal Harper's eyes landed on Jillian. The Hamilton's gave no introduction to her.

"Hello, I'm Sophies dearest friend, Jillian Parker," Jillian introduced herself, smirking at Sophie as she did. "My husband and I live over at Pier Seventeen."

"Oh, yes. I remember it was up for sell last year. What a tragic thing too. To buy land in Kosher Harbor one day and then to have it almost completely destroyed by Hurricane Candi when she unexpectedly hit." Principal Harper shook his head in disbelief before continuing. "A lot of families suffered. How did your home hold up?"

Sandy started to speak but was cut off by Winston. "You know who suffered the most? Me. That's who. That hurricane hit my doorsteps first. If it wasn't for our mansion slowing the storm down, I bet all of Kosher Harbor would have been wiped off the map. Damn storm nearly took out our entire barn. Had to make some modifications. Made it bigger of course and reinforced it. Reinforced the entire home too. Next storm that comes through won't stand a chance against my property, isn't that right Sophie?"

"Melvin, go play on the playground with your little friends. This is grownup talk," Sophie ordered the boy. Melvin nodded and ran off towards the playground, even though the boy didn't have any friends. "I hate it when children eavesdrop. But yes, our land and five piers were hit the hardest. That storm came from the southeast, so of course we got it first. If it would have hit the lower-class part of Kosher Harbor before our side, those trashy trailers would have been blown away," she snapped her fingers right in Principal Harper's face, "just like that. They're lucky they got the tail end of it."

"Well, let's not forget about the ones who lost their lives. Afterall, it's why we're having this fish fry. To celebrate their lives," Jillian spoke softly.

"Of course, Jillian. Just because we're rich doesn't mean we don't have feelings. Honestly, the things that come out of your mouth sometimes."

Jillian's eyes narrowed and she had to bite her tongue. "I'll be in the cafeteria. That is where we'll be cooking, I presume?" she asked Principal Harper.

"Yes, when you go inside there will be a hallway on your right. Take it half way down and then turn left. At the end of that hall is the cafeteria entrance."

"I'll see you inside shortly Sophie. I'll start setting up," Jillian said, grabbing a cooler from the trunk before making her way to the school's doors.

"I apologize, Principal Harper. Jillian visits our fish stand and I think she's become obsessed with me. I hardly know her. We are *not* friends. But Evelyn has fallen ill and we didn't want to disappoint the citizens of Kosher Harbor, so Jillian volunteered to help when she overheard me talking about it yesterday. I hope you don't mind," Sophie said, playing with the strand of pearls that hung around her neck. She batted her eyes at Principal Harper. "I just think it's odd that she wanted to volunteer to help. She doesn't even have children. And with them being new to town, I'm sure they don't have friends or family here."

Winston grabbed Sophie's hand and gave it a gentle squeeze. "Perhaps this is her way of trying to make new friends. You're always suspicious of new people. Remember you were suspicious of me when we first met?" Winston planted a kiss on his wife's lips and their tongues tangled into one another.

Principal Harper looked uncomfortable with the sudden public display of affection. "Do you need any help with the other coolers?" he asked, hoping they would stop kissing.

CHAPTER 14

A high-pitched screech echoed throughout the auditorium. Several people that were seated at the plethora of lunch tables, which were crammed into the elementary school's gym, squeezed their eyes shut and slammed the palms of their hands over their ears to protect them from the sound that blasted from the speakers surrounding them.

Principal Harper took a few steps away from one of the heavy, black speakers that stood on the edge of the stage. "Sorry about that," he declared as he spoke into the microphone again. "I want to start off by thanking everybody who came out to today's fish fry. It's been a rough year of recovery for the citizens of Kosher Harbor.

That includes myself. It's been just over a year since Hurricane Candi hit us. Just over a year since many of us suffered significant damages from the storm. Just over a year since some of us lost our homes entirely. Not only our homes..." Principal Harper's voice cracked. He cleared his throat and started again. "Not only our homes, but also our loved ones. Quite a few of you in this gymnasium lost loved ones. Neighbors. Friends. Family."

Quietness loomed over the crowd as his last words lingered in the air. Principal Harper looked at the citizens gathered in front of him. Some of them met his eyes with their own. Others kept their heads bowed as they quietly cried tears of sorrow from the fresh memories of death that touched their hearts not so long ago.

"Death is hard. Life is harder. The ones who were taken from us will never be forgotten. They'll continue to live on in our memories; in our hearts. No one sitting in this room is alone. We still have community. We still have each other. Nothing can destroy our community. Not even a hurricane!"

The crowd erupted in cheers. Several people stood up and whooped and cheered. Everyone was clapping. Principal Harper was beaming with gratitude that his speech touched the citizens of Kosher Harbor.

Principal Harper tapped his fingers on top of the microphone, trying to get the crowd to calm back down. "Just another quick word, folks. I want to give a special thanks to the Hamilton's for providing all the fish for today's fish fry!"

The community erupted in cheers and clapping once again. Maverick Tucker rushed the stage and stomped his feet as he climbed the few steps. He yanked the microphone out of Principal Harper's hand. "And a huge shoutout to me and my wife Florence, for providing all of the fixins!" he yelled into the microphone with spit flying from his mouth. "You'll need our delicious, homemade coleslaw and potatoes to get the taste of Winston's rancid fish out of your mouths!"

Principal Harper tugged the microphone back from his hands and cringed as saliva oozed down the side of it.

The auditorium doors flung open and in walked Celeste, the town's crazed psychic. Locks of curly hair stuck out from a giant lime green turban that she wore. Both wrists were decorated in a dozen bangles and all ten fingers bared rings with colorful stones set in them. They were obviously costume jewelry; nothing of true value. Sophie Hamilton wouldn't be caught dead in any of the jewels that Celeste wore.

Celeste clutched the shawl that was around her shoulders as she walked to the stage. She twisted her neck, side to side, looking over the crowd as if she was searching for someone in particular. She climbed the steps, almost tripping over her own feet as she did. She ignored the microphone completely and the two men who stood before her. She faced the crowd and let her shawl drop to the floor as she extended both of her hands outward, as if she was being crucified.

"Hear me!" she bellowed. "I come to warn you all!"

"We know, you're a kook!" someone yelled from the crowd. Several others laughed at the comment.

Celeste ignored the comment and continued as if she wasn't interrupted. "I dreamed a dark dream of death last night. The vibrations of the future shook my body to its core and as I woke with a cold sweat, the stars were singing to me."

Celeste's hands begun to convulse, still

outstretched as far as her decorated fingers could reach. The town watched on as she started to spin in circles like a child would. "Two of you will become stars tonight," she declared, still spinning round and round.

"Enough of this nonsense," Principal Harper spoke to himself. He grabbed Celeste by her arm and started to drag her off stage. She didn't resist as he guided her down the steps.

Maverick Tucker ran ahead of them to open the gymnasium doors and just as Principal Harper was urging Celeste to exit, her body rebuked and she spun around to face the room again. "The first will float to the sky and the second will falsely fall. You have been warned. You were warned about Candi, but no one listened and you all paid the price. Heed my warning and save yourself!"

Maverick and Principal Harper pushed the town's physic outside and slammed the doors shut behind her and her crazy prophecy.

CHAPTER 15

The smell was intoxicating. Fried fish and chips, along with other fixins hypnotized the citizens of Kosher Harbor into a feeding frenzy. They lined up on two sides of the room and plate after plate was being dished out to them. Winston and Sophie Hamilton were dishing out the main course of battered and fried fish, alongside Jillian Parker, who plated catfish and fresh, homemade fish sticks and ketchup for the children. Maverick Tucker, his wife Florance, and Principal Harper were across the room shoveling out all the fixin's. The Tucker's served homemade hushpuppies, coleslaw, potato salad, and fries that left a puddle of grease on the plate.

"What'll it be?" Sophie asked the next person in

line. It wasn't just the next person in line. It was the last person in line. "I've got cod, my husband is serving the halibut, and miss priss down there has the catfish and fish sticks," she said to the woman waiting to be fed.

Jillian couldn't help but smile at Sophie's remark. Only a couple more hours left of this and she would have another pocket full of cash and would end her odd friendship with Sophie once and for all. Jillian knew the woman was as crazy as Celeste, maybe more. But she needed the money. So, she endured the punishment.

The woman took her time and pondered. She looked at each type of fish that was offered in front of her. She shifted her weight to her good leg. She was supporting herself up with a cane. She sighed a relief as if she was in pain from waiting in line. She leaned forward and took a whiff of each fish.

"I do not have all day. Make a decision," Sophie ordered the woman without an ounce of kindness in her snobby tone.

"Don't you fucking talk to me like that Sophie Hamilton. I'll reach across this table and strangle the life out of you right in front of the entire damn town. And there's not a damn person in here that would or *could* stop me!" The woman raised her hand up and Sophie flinched. But she wasn't going to hit her. Instead, she grabbed her hair that was in a single long braid that laid in front of her shoulder and moved it back behind her back.

"Now I stood in this line long enough. And I got a bad knee. Damn doctor in this godforsaken town won't do a thing to help me out either. Keeps rescheduling my appointment. I've had enough of everyone in Kosher Harbor thinking they're better than big, old Cecilia Claiborne. Things are gonna change and they're gonna change right now. So, you can patiently wait while I make my decision on what type of fish I'll be taking back to my husband tonight. He just came back home today after four years and I'm gonna feed my man tonight!"

Sophie glared at Cecilia. "You must be new to town. I would be very careful at how you speak to me and my husband."

Jillian intervened. "Sophie. Winston. I'll help out Mrs. Claiborne. You two can go and eat. I don't mind." Jillian gave a smile at Cecilia and Cecilia returned the smile with one of her own. Without another word, the Hamilton's left.

"I apologize for her. She's…"

"A bitch?" Cecilia said without hesitation.

Jillian laughed out loud. It was the first time she laughed today and she let her shoulders relax. She didn't know she was so tensed up until now. "I'm Jillian Parker. Welcome to Kosher Harbor."

"I know who you are. I run into you at the fish market every once in a while. Why doesn't anyone ever remember me in this damn town?"

"I'm so sorry. My husband and I have only lived here for just over a year. It must have slipped my mind."

"It's alright. I'm used to it."

"You said your husband just came back?"

"Yes. He's deathly ill. He looks like shit. I think some fresh fish will do him good."

"Do you know what kind you want? I promise I'm not trying to rush you." Jillian said.

"The Hamilton's are providing all this for free?" Cecilia asked. "Why don't you go ahead and take what you want and I'll take everything else home for Brenden and me to snack on for the next couple of days."

Jillian laughed again. "Yes, it's all free. And that sounds like a great idea to me. Less cleanup."

Cecilia had stacks of fish on a single plate but it

was too heavy. It slipped and she went to steady it with her other hand and accidently dropped her 7-Eleven big gulp cup. The plastic cup split open and Mountain Dew spilled all over her shoes. "Son of a bitch!" the woman roared. The gymnasium went quiet and everyone turned to look at her.

"Please, let me help you carry all this." Jillian took the plate from Cecilia to hold and the outlandish woman took it as a sign to fill up another plate of food to take home with her; one for her and the other for her dying husband.

CHAPTER 16

Jillian had enough. She was dead on her feet and listening to Sophie treat that poor old woman like dirt beneath her shoe had almost pushed Jillian over the edge. Jillian wished she could finish a bottle of wine off when she got home but she let that idea fade away into nothingness as she inhaled deeply, held her breath for a few moments, and exhaled slowly. She was pregnant and so downing a bottle of wine while reading a good book was out of the question. Well, at least the wine part was out of the question. She decided she would stop at the local book store before she headed home.

"Jillian!" Sophie yelled the name, snapping her out of the daydream of browsing for a new thriller series to get lost into. "Jillian, I'm not paying you to just stand around and look pretty. That's my job."

"What do you need now, Sophie?"

"First of all, young lady, I need you to adjust that tone to a more pleasant one."

Jillian waited. She knew if she opened her mouth that whatever words came out would cost her the other half of the money she was promised. She blinked twice and forced a smile. "How can I help?" she spoke the words with a harsh kindness that only her mother would recognize from her teenage years.

"That's better. Now, Principal Harper just informed us that the panel of judges are gathering and we have just over a half an hour to serve them."

Jillian sighed. "But we're done serving food. Everyone has eaten."

Sophie clutched her pearls. "Everyone has eaten? Jillian! We need three more dishes. Three dishes are being served to the judges. Did you forget about the competition? Were you dropped on your head as a baby?" Sophie took a few steps back, still visibly upset and still clutching her pearl necklace. "Jillian, I know you have pregnancy brain, but could you please pull it together before you give me a heart attack?"

"You didn't say anything to me about a competition. I did everything you asked of me." Jillian said with conviction.

Winston approached the two ladies and placed his hand on Sophie's lower back. "Darling, time is of the essence."

"Truer now than ever, my love. Jillian just told me she doesn't want to be part of the community anymore. She said she doesn't want to help us cook for the judges. So, it'll just be the two of us."

"That's not what I said, Sophie."

Winston and Sophie stared at Jillian, unmoving.

"Fine." Jillian said. "How can I help?"

And with that, the trio, Jillian being the third wheel, headed to the kitchen to prepare their dishes with the other fish market vendors who had entered the competition. As they prepped, fried, and plated their dishes to serve, the three judges, Principal Harper, Maverick Tucker, and Dr. David Hanus were sitting down at a long table that was placed onto the stage. In the center of the table sat a pitcher of ice water. Beside each judge was a glass, napkin, silverware, and microphones.

Principal Harper grabbed his microphone and started to speak before realizing it wasn't turned on. He flipped the switch on its bottom and stood up this time, walking in front of the table to address the community of Kosher Harbor.

"I'd like to take this opportunity to once again thank everyone who came out today. I hope no one is still hungry. We're about to start the cookoff to see which fish vendor is the best! Are you excited, Kosher Harbor?" Principal Harper tried his best to rally the crowd. Most people cheered and clapped. Others seemed to be ready to leave but didn't want to be the first to do it.

"We'll do a quick introduction to our judges before we start. You all already know me as Principal Harper of Kosher Harbor Elementary. And that's why I'm one of the judges, just like I have always been in previous years. Behind me is Maverick Tucker, one of the best fishermen in Kosher Harbor."

"*The* best fisherman. I only just retired from it." Mr. Tucker interrupted.

"Yes, if you say so. This is Mr. Tucker's first time judging at the annual fish fry. Where was I? Oh, yes. And beside Mr. Tucker sits Dr. Hanus. This is his first time judging at the annual fish fry as well. Dr. Hanus has his own practice here in town.

Dr. Hanus stood up and fumbled with his microphone. "Let it be known that I am accepting new patients and I also accept all insurances, including Medicaid and Medicare."

"He's the worse damn doctor I've ever had!" Cecelia yelled from her seat.

"Who said that?" Dr. Hanus demanded as he searched the crowd for the culprit.

"Let me guess, you forgot about big old Cecelia Claiborne too? I was at your office last week, remember? You told me I needed to lose fifty pounds before you would replace my knee! Who can lose fifty pounds with all this free food? Who can lose fifty pounds when you can get sixty-four ounces of cold pop for just sixty-nine cents?"

"Ma'am, I cannot discuss medical information in front of these people. It's against HIPAA law."

"Screw HIPAA and screw you too!" Cecelia yelled, stuffing another piece of fried fish in her mouth.

"Alright, here comes the first round!" Principal

Harper interrupted, as a couple entered back into the gymnasium from a side door while carrying three covered platters.

Principal Harper took his seat and the couple placed a platter in front of each judge. They introduced themselves to the crowd and said what they were serving to the judges. One after another, the lids came off and the smell of fish wafered through the air once again. Each judge picked up their fork and took their first bite. They chewed as they savored the flavors and tilted their heads, looking at one another. Maverick took his pad of paper and pencil and circled a few of the categories.

Dr. Hanus looked his paper over completely from top to bottom before starting at the top again. He hesitantly circled line after line, then erased a couple circles and changed them. He didn't feel as confident as Maverick did with his answers.

Principal Harper took a second then a third bite from his fish before he was satisfied with what he was tasting. He grabbed his paper and filled it out, just as the others did.

Each judge poured water into their glass and gulped it down, rinsing the fishy flavors from their mouths for the next round. The judges ate a few bites from plate, after plate, after plate. After each dish they would rinse their mouth out with water to help remove the flavors from the last dish they just consumed. It wasn't an eating contest; they didn't finish a single dish. Rather, they took a single bite, maybe two, before judging the next dish that was placed in front of them.

The time came for the Hamilton's and Jillian to present their dish to the judges. Winston, followed by Sophie and then Jillian, took the stage steps and presented their plates in front of each of the judges. Winston placed his dish in front of Principal Harper. Sophie placed her dish next to his in front of Dr. Hanus. Jillian copied their motions and placed her dish in front of Maverick Tucker. Principal Harper and Dr. Hanus smiled as their dishes were uncovered. Maverick Tucker snorted out loud, implying that the dish was subpar.

Winston looked to Sophie and she gave her husband a smile and grabbed his hand to hold in her own. The Hamilton's and Jillian stepped aside to watch with everyone else as the judges ate their prepared dish.

They each chewed with their mouths closed for a few moments. Maverick cleared his throat and shifted in his seat. Sophie and Winston looked at the residents of Kosher Harbor, still seated and watching them all on stage, waiting for them to announce a winner; an announcement that would never come.

Principal Harper was checking boxes on the paper in front of him. Dr. Hanus was licking his lips and nodding his head, clearly delighted at what he just shoveled into his mouth. Maverick Tucker grunted and stood to his feet. He started making choking noises and grabbed his chest. Everyone turned to look at him. No one moved. The choking man was sitting next to the town's doctor. Surely, he would be fine.

"Are you alright, Tucker?" Principal Harper asked his fellow judge.

Dr. Hanus stood up, ready to take action. It was too late. Maverick began to foam at the mouth like a rabid dog. Dr. Hanus actually took a step *away* from him, afraid he might catch whatever the man had. But Maverick wasn't sick. He was dying. Maverick lurched forward, grabbing Dr. Hanus by the arm. More of the white foam bubbled from his lips. He coughed, still choking. Dr. Hanus tried to get his arm away from the man, clearly afraid of what was happening to him. It was as if Dr.

Hanus thought he was going rabid with rabies!

Maverick's hold on the doctor's arm was still strong. He released him for a split second to grab Dr. Hanus by his shirt collar instead, pulling their bodies closer together. Maverick let out a cry of agony and Dr. Hanus returned it with a scream of fear of his own. Maverick pulled on the doctor's shirt, shaking the man. He needed his help. He was dying and the doctor wasn't doing a damn thing to help him!

Maverick's eyes went dead and his legs gave out as he fell onto the table, pulling Dr. Hanus down with him. Their weight was too much and the table snapped and broke beneath them. Remains of dead fish and glass fell on top of the pair.

"Help me! Somebody, help me!" Dr. Hanus screamed out loud to the citizens of Kosher Harbor.

Winston and Sophie were still holding hands. They both gave one another a gentle squeeze as their neighbor died right in front of them and the entire town.

CHAPTER 17

Evelyn knew the endgame to her story. Winston had shuffled the deck and Sophie was the one to cut. She needed to play her cards that were delt to her carefully and deliberately. She wore her poker face for years now and now it was time to go all in. She knew her in-laws, Winston and Sophie, had stacked the deck against her when her husband Carter was killed. She knew the story of his boat being attacked by a shark was a cock and bull cover story her in-laws made up. She knew deep down that they killed their own firstborn son. It was hardly the first time they killed their own flesh and blood. And Evelyn knew they would never stop. What if they decided to kill her? What if they decided to kill Melvin? The possibility is even greater now that they used up a good chunk of bodies from the barn the other day for today's fish fry.

Evelyn packed a duffle bag with a couple outfits for herself and her son, Melvin. She stuffed an envelope full of cash she had stashed away into her pocket and grabbed her car keys. She left the house without locking the door behind her. She tossed the duffle bag in the truck and slammed it shut. Once she was behind the wheel, she put the peddle to the floor and sped off, making her way to the center of Kosher Harbor to her destination: Pier Seventeen, home of Mitchell and Jillian Parker.

As she drove, Evelyn glanced out the driver window. The water slammed into the rocks and the light bounced off the water, creating a rainbow effect for a split second before disappearing into nothingness. It gave her hope. Hope that better days were ahead. Once they would escape Kosher Harbor, they could finally live a good life without murderous secrets. Evelyn knew she couldn't go to the police. She knew Winston had a few of them on his payroll. She could never let her little boy be exposed to the ugly truth of the Hamilton lifestyle of lies and murder.

First, she had a game to finish playing. She parked the car a block away and followed the sidewalk to the Parker's home. She went around back and peered through a window. She never been here before, but Sophie had given her the address with special instructions the night before. She hoped in doing this last wicked deed for Sophie and Winston, that she would be able to leave in peace without being followed. Scratch my back, I'll scratch yours. At least, that's what Evelyn was hoping how it would go down. But hope in Kosher Harbor was a dangerous thing that rarely stuck around.

Was framing Jillian wrong? Of course it was. Did Evelyn care? Of course not. The only thing Evelyn cared about was getting her son away from his grandparents and escaping Kosher Harbor once and for all.

The front door was unlocked. It was the far side of Kosher Harbor that was unsafe. The middle was better and most people left doors unlocked during the daylight hours. Evelyn entered the home without knocking. No cars were parked out front. Most people in this town were at the fish fry stuffing their faces full of fish provided by the Hamilton's themselves. The same fish that fed off human flesh. It was sickening to think of. Evelyn only ate fish from others that was already cooked for her at restaurants. She never ate the fish that was caught within a mile of the Hamilton property. It was all tainted.

Evelyn glanced at the buffet table that was against the wall next to the front door. There was an eight by ten photograph of Mitchell and Jullian on their wedding day. *How sweet*, Evelyn thought to herself.

It made her sick to her stomach thinking that she was about to frame this innocent pregnant woman in order to protect her own child. But she hoped Jillian would forgive her one day. There was that damn word again: hope. It was a lost cause in this hell hole of a town. *Oh well. Life goes on, if you do what's necessary to survive*, Evelyn thought to herself.

Evelyn stopped thinking. She went into work mode. She didn't think about the lives she was about to destroy. She didn't think about the innocent unborn baby that would suffer from the task she was about to perform, which was ripping a family apart with lies and secrets.

Evelyn took a pair of gloves out of her pocket and put them on. She proceeded to pull out a small unmarked, tinted glass jar from her other pocket and placed it in the kitchen cabinet above the stainless-steel fridge. She thought it was filled with grounded down human bones. The same bones from dead relatives that had the unfortunate luck of not being born first. What Evelyn didn't know, was that this bottle was half full of arsenic, a silvery gray substance. It was the same arsenic that Winston used to kill his own son; her husband eight years ago.

These people are sick. How can a family do that to a person? She thought to herself, examining the glass bottle of poison. It baffled her. She quickly realized that she was part of *those people* and stopped thinking again. She wondered how long it would take her to look at her own face in a mirror after this. She probably would never look at herself again. At least her son would be safe. That's all that mattered to Evelyn.

After planting the jar of evidence, she made her way upstairs to their bedroom. More wedding photos lined the wall as she walked up the steps. She tried not to look at their happy faces. The upstairs hallway seemed tight as she walked to the bedroom at the end of the hall. A reading nook was built in the hallway. Three shelves were lined up with books and little trinkets. A small table with an oversized porcelain lamp with hand painted trees sat beside a pastel blue chair with a high back. It looked cozy. *Who had time to read these days?* Evelyn thought to herself as she swung their bedroom door open.

Evelyn made her way over to the dresser that had a large mirror attached to its top and pulled open the top drawer. She knew this is where Jillian would keep her clothes. The woman always had the dresser with the mirror. She grabbed a handful of panties and shut the drawer back.

She was done with the Parker home. Now she needed to pay a visit to the Tucker's to plant the fake evidence of an affair and her job was over.

CHAPTER 18

"Jillian Parker, you are under arrest for the murder of Maverick Tucker."

"Murder? What are you doing?" Jillian yelled at the officer. Her arms fought against being pulled behind her back and put into cuffs. She was innocent. What were they doing? She didn't kill Maverick. He was old. He must have had a heart attack. Why was she being arrested? Jillian didn't understand why the entire town was whispering about her. She didn't understand why she was being put into handcuffs when she did nothing wrong. This wasn't murder. This was chaos and they were all wrong.

"I didn't do anything wrong. What are you

doing?" Jillian yelled at the police officer, still resisting.

It had happened all so fast. Maverick was on stage, eating. And then he was falling over with foamy saliva spewing from his mouth. Did he have an allergic reaction? What else could have happened to the man?

"Stop resisting!" Officer Edwards yelled.

What was she doing? She was so confused. Jillian let her arms go limp, no longer resisting. She was one hundred percent innocent. This was just a bad misunderstanding and everything would be cleared up by morning. A bad day and a bad night. That's all this was. She would answer all their questions truthfully and this would all be behind her by tomorrow afternoon. Worst case scenario, Mitch would hire a lawyer and she would be proven innocent and all charges would be dropped.

"You have the right to remain silent. Anything you say can and will be used against you in a court of law. You have a right to an attorney. If you cannot afford an attorney, one will be appointed to you," Officer Edwards said in a robotic tone to Jillian Parker.

"I didn't kill anyone! I'm innocent! I swear to you. Call my husband. I want my husband!" Jillian yelled.

No one listened to her.

Officer Edwards placed his hand on the top of Jillian's head as he placed her into the back of his police cruiser, not wanting to bump her head. She no longer resisted. She seemed annoyed by the situation, which was odd. Most people who are caught act smug. But not Jillian. She was playing the victim.

Officer Edwards knew better. After watching Maverick foam at the mouth and drop dead in front of the entire town, it was quite clear that the man was poisoned. The only question was who did it? It only took a few minutes of talking to Winston and Sophie to declare that Jillian was the one who prepared his food and killed him. Shut and close case. An easy day at the office. A bad day sure, but an easy day nonetheless. Officer Edwards dreaded the paperwork. Murder was page after page of reports he would have to write up and turn in. He wished he hadn't even come to the fish fry tonight.

"Thank you for your cooperation, Mr. and Mrs. Hamilton," Officer Edwards said to the happy couple.

"Oh, you're welcome, young man," Winston responded. "Anything for the police force. This town couldn't run without your hard work and dedication." I'll tell your chief you done an excellent job today." Winston gave the police officer a pat on the back to show approval of his quick arrest.

"I just cannot believe that Jillian tricked me. I'm usually a good judge of character, but she threw a fast one over us these past few days. I had no idea she could be so evil." Sophie held her nose up a little higher when she spoke lies about other people. "That's what I get for trusting strangers. Not everyone in Kosher Harbor can be trusted. It's obvious now that new people who come to this town do not always have our best interest at heart. I just hope that God can forgive her soul for being filled with such evilness. And to think she tried to blame this on me! I assure you I she was the one who insisted on preparing Maverick's dish. She handpicked the slice of fish and did the seasoning. Neither of us lifted a finger to help her. She insisted she had it under control. Did you search her pockets? I bet she has evidence on her. Did you check her station she used in the cafeteria?" Sophie's voice started to sound frantic as she touched her fingertips to her pearl necklace and with the other hand, she wiped tears away that did not exist from her eyes.

"Indeed, we will do that. And how long have you known her again?" Officer Edwards asked Sophie as he took a small notepad out again.

"Well, Jillian has shopped from our stand for months now. She always been asking me questions about how to cook and she recently told me she was with child. I believe she has been under a lot of stress because she was worried about how her husband would react about her being pregnant. I accidently let it slip late last night and her husband did seem quite upset now that I think about it. You don't suppose Maverick was the real father? Maybe that's why she didn't want her husband to know she was pregnant. Is that why she killed him? To get rid of all the evidence of an affair?"

"We're not sure yet. But we will get to the bottom of her motive," Officer Edwards confirmed. He scribbled a few more notes down.

"Oh, I'm certain a man of your caliber will get her confession within the day. Please, let me know if you need any more information about Jillian. I will drop whatever I'm doing and come straight over to the station, if need be," Sophie promised with a smile and wink as she slipped a hundred-dollar bill in the officer's hand.

Officer Edwards hastily stuck the money into his pocket. The last time he accepted money from the

Hamilton's was a few days after Hurricane Candi. Winston gave him two hundred dollars to take the body off his hands that he had found. Cold hard cash and no paperwork was exactly what Officer Edwards liked.

CHAPTER 19

More police officers and EMTs arrived on scene. A firetruck even pulled up with its sirens blaring. The police officers took photographs as evidence and the EMTs loaded Maverick's body into the ambulance while his wife sobbed hysterically. She refused to ride along with the corpse of what used to be her husband just moments ago.

After taking many photographs from many angles, while most the town continued to watch, they finally informed Principal Harper that he could start to clean up.

"Clean up? What do you mean? I'm not touching the tables or the chairs. There could be poison fragments left on them! What if I get infected?"

"You're a school. You should have gloves somewhere, right?" Officer Edwards commented.

"Excuse me. Excuse me!" Mitchell Parker yelled, making his way through the crowd and up to the stage; up to the crime scene. 'What happened? Where is Jillian? I got tied up at work and couldn't make it here until now. Someone told me they arrested her!"

"Oh, are you Mitchell?" Principal Harper inquired.

"Yes, I am. Now what happened to my wife? Is she alright?"

"Is she alright? Is *she* alright? Your wife killed a man, Mr. Parker!" Principal Harper yelled, clearly disgusted with what had happened on school grounds.

The two men stared at one another in silence.

Winston saw the opportunity and stepped in. "If I may, Principal Harper, it has been a long day. Why don't you let us speak to the crowd and then we will clean things up before we leave. Go home. Your staff and students will need to hear from you come Monday morning. Get some rest and then you can write a speech. Let us deal with all this."

Principal Harper looked at the broken table and

mess of chairs and scattered food. It was sickening to look at. He wanted to escape this place. But he felt he had a responsibility to stay. This was his school after all.

"Trust me, nothing you say now will change what just happened. Let the town settle down before you address them. Let the parents speak to their children about what they witnessed before you do. It's what's best for the children." Winston said, placing his hand on his shoulder and giving it a gentle squeeze.

"You're right, Winston. I think I will go. Thank you, for everything." Principal Harper gave another quick glance at Mitchell and turned his back to leave.

"Mitchell Parker, my name is Winston Hamilton."

"I know who you are. You're Sophie's husband."

'Yes, Sophie is *my* wife." Winston corrected him.

"What happened here?"

"I believe your questions need to be directed to the police. They're the ones with all the correct information. Anything other than that is hearsay."

Mitchell shook his head. If he was going to get the answers he was looking for, he needed to go to the police station. That's where his wife was being taken and that's where he needed to be. Mitchell didn't say anything else. He turned to leave and saw that the entire town was now looking at him and they were all whispering.

"Winston," Sophie said. "Let me speak to everyone here. It will be better coming from me. The town interacts more with me. They're more comfortable with me. This requires a woman's touch. These people are on edge right now. We must treat this delicately. Otherwise, it could all backfire on us."

Winston nodded. He walked over to the microphone and picked it up off the floor and handed it to Sophie.

Sophie placed her fingertips up to her pearl necklace and inhaled. "Residents of Kosher Harbor, I would first like to apologize for what we all just witnessed. It's true, Maverick Tucker was just murdered. It seems Jillian Parker, a somewhat new resident to Kosher Harbor, had put something in his dish that she prepared for him today."

Sophie paused to let that lie sink in before continuing. "I want to let all of you know that were not friends with Jillian. She was a customer of mine, like many of you are, and I hope will continue to be for many years.

Jillian came to me a couple days ago and informed me that she was pregnant. She said her husband Mitchell and she was having financial difficulties since Hurricane Candi. I mean, aren't we all? I just wanted to be a good person. So, I offered her a little cash to help out today. We didn't need the help. But I thought it was the neighborly thing to do." Sophie took her husband's hand into her own. "I spoke with one of the officers' moments ago, and they informed me that Jillian might have been *involved* with Maverick. A scandal that she clearly didn't want her husband to find out about... But I don't want to spread rumors. All I want is understanding. My husband and I are the victims here. We had no idea Jillian was using us to get close enough to poison Maverick. My husband and Maverick have been friends for many years. They went to grade school together. He is also a victim in all of this, may God rest his soul."

Sophie turned and gave her husband a hug in front of the crowd that was listening to her every last word. "With that being said, this was the only time Jillian Parker has ever worked with us. And we promise you that no outsider will ever endanger your lives again by using us."

Sophie finished speaking and wiped fake tears away from her eyes once again. She turned around and gave Winston a quick peck on the cheek, dropping the microphone from her hand.

CHAPTER 20

Cleaning the crime scene took less than half an hour. A handful of people from the crowd volunteered to help. Mostly because they wanted to get a closer look of the mess, not because they actually wanted to help. It seemed as if another disaster had struck Kosher Harbor today. Last year, it was Hurricane Candi. And on the anniversary, a murder in front of the whole damn town. Kosher Harbor Times Union would have this story on its frontpage by tomorrow morning.

"Do you have all your belongings, Melvin?"
"Yes, Grandma. I didn't bring anything with me."
"Alright, go ahead and hop in the car."
"Where's mommy? Melvin asked.

"She's at home. She's sick, remember?"

Melvin climbed in the backseat of the car and buckled himself in. "I don't like it when I get sick."

"She will be fine. She is probably already feeling better. Don't forget to buckle your seatbelt."

Melvin thought to himself that it had been a very exciting week for him. He enjoyed seeing the man die on stage. He wished he had friends to tell them about the naked dead bodies inside the barn but was glad he didn't. He wasn't sure if he would be able to keep the secret if he did have friends. He hoped he could see the frozen bodies again sometime soon. Maybe the bodies in the barn could be his friends. Melvin wondered if he asked his grandpa if he would be allowed to visit them again. He didn't care what his mom would say. Grandpa was the real boss.

Winston started the car and the Hamilton's made their way home. The school quickly disappeared in the rearview mirror just as fast as their remorse of the murder of their neighbor, Maverick Tucker.

They pulled into the long driveway that led to the Hamilton manor. The big white house was just as they left it. In the distance, you could see waves splash up against the rocks just behind the ominous, old barn which held the family's biggest secret: the deceased citizens of Kosher Harbor were hanging on hooks, naked and frozen; waiting to be used as fish bait.

Evelyn came out of the house and Melvin ran up to her. "I'm glad you're feeling better, Mommy."

"Thank you. You're so sweet." Evelyn paused. "You're so innocent in all of this, aren't you? I love you, Melvin."

Melvin looked up to his mom's face, hearing the worry within her words. "I love you too, Mommy," the boy lied to his mother.

"Did you do it?" Sophie asked Evelyn.

"Yes. It's done. And it's the last thing I'm every doing for either of you. I'm done. I'm washing my hands of all of this. I'm washing my hands of this family. We're leaving."

Winston turned to Sophie. "Go inside and make us up some lemonade. We'll be in shortly, my love."

Sophie nodded her head once and passed Evelyn without looking at her.

"Melvin, go to your room," Winston ordered his grandson.

"He's not going anywhere," Evelyn firmly said.

"Now!" Winston yelled this time.

Melvin knew something was wrong. He knew his grandpa was mad at his mom and not him. She must have done something bad.

"Evelyn grabbed Melvin by the hand and started walking towards the other car.

Winston sidestepped and now stood between Evelyn and her means of escape. Melvin tried to pull away from Evelyn's grasp she had on him.

"Move," Evelyn demanded.

"We give you a roof over your head. We give you a job in our family business. We help you raise our grandson after our son tragically died and you tell me to move?"

Tears trickled from Evelyn's eyes, running down her cheeks. "A roof over my head but not a place I can ever call home. A job that involves murdering innocent people. And there was no tragic accident. I know the truth. You killed your own firstborn son!"

Winston narrowed his eyes. Evelyn started to walk past him. Her bravery was her downfall. Winston grabbed her by her throat and pushed her backwards towards the house. "You're not going anywhere!" the old man shouted.

Melvin yanked his arm away from his mother's grip. He knew she was in trouble and he didn't want anything to do with anyone who upset grandpa. He was the only one who understood him.

Evelyn yanked away from her father-in-law's grasp. She had to escape. They were going to kill her, just like they did Carter. She had to escape so she could save their son! Evelyn ran. She ran as fast as she could away from him. She had to escape these monsters. The only way to escape was the water. She knew she could outswim her in-laws. On land they could easily follow in a car. They had no time to get the keys to chase her in the boat. She would have to return for her son another night. She headed toward the brown barn, just passing the end of the house. She planned to jump once she reached the edge of the cliff.

Evelyn groaned when she heard the squeak of the back screen door open. She knew Sophie was now behind her as well.

"Do it!" Winston yelled.

Do what? Evelyn thought. She had no time to look

behind her. She needed to make it to the water.

Sophie pulled the trigger. An arrow shot out of the harpoon gun the elderly woman was holding. With precision aim, Sophie did not miss. It shot straight through Evelyn. In and out. A clean shot, minus the blood.

Evelyn collapsed with a scream. Sophie yanked back on the rope that was attached to the harpoon for good measure. Evelyn laid in agony. There was no escape. The edge of the cliff was just yards away. If she had ran five seconds earlier…

Winston took his time catching up to Evelyn. Once he did, he kneeled down beside her. "I told you; you're not going anywhere. And neither is our grandson.

CHAPTER 21

The sky grew darker much faster than Evelyn thought was possible. She was laying on top of the butcher block inside the kitchen looking outside through the screen door. Sophie had cut the rope and removed the harpoon that was lodged through her. How she was still alive, she did not know. She felt dead. She wished she was.

She could see the edge of the barn in the distance. She was told it used to be bright red and full of life. Now she figured that was also a lie that was told to her. That barn only brought death. It was almost over and she was happy at the thought of dying. What did not sit well with her was the thought of leaving her son with these maniacs. That, and having her body be eaten away by fish.

That thought alone made her want to vomit.

Evelyn turned her head away from the screen door. She didn't want to see the brown barn that was full of frozen bodies of the deceased that were lost from Hurricane Candi. She didn't want to watch her last sun set. She only wanted to see Melvin's face one last time. She wanted to assure her son that she loved him. She wanted to tell him to stay strong without her. She wanted to tell him to run away and never look back.

"We told you a long time ago to never speak of Carter again. Did you forget? We told you there would be consequences," Winston spoke from the corner of the kitchen with his back facing Evelyn. The sound of metal sharpening metal could be heard as he spoke.

"Carter's death was your fault," he continued. "Falling in love is one thing. Sophie and I fell in love with one another when we were younger than Carter and you. But Sophie learned her place a long time. The same place that you should have learned. But you never did. You tried to convince him that his family was evil. You tried to convince him to leave us. You tried to turn our son against us and deny us from ever meeting our grandchild."

Evelyn laid there, listening. She did not try to escape. She was too weak to move. It was hopeless. She laid bleeding on the butcher block. She wished death would take her. She wished she would bleed out completely before Winston made his first cut. She feared once he started, he would drag it out, just to torture her. Her death would not be swift. It would last a lifetime. She was sure of it. Perhaps she had already died.

"Is this Hell?" she asked with a weak voice.

Winston turned around, holding the freshly sharpened hatchet in his hand. "No. This is Kosher Harbor."

A gust of wind blew through the screen door and into the kitchen. Winston walked to the door and shut and locked them both. The screams would begin soon and he didn't want to disturb the neighbors.

He turned his attention back to Evelyn. "He wrote a letter to us. Explaining that he understood why we do what we do. He even promised to visit on holidays. But he said you would leave him if he didn't leave us. His death was entirely your fault."

"I want to see my son. Please, let me see him one last time. Where is he?"

"Yes, I thought you would ask for the boy. He's upstairs with his lovely grandmother. She's calming him down because you caused a scene when we returned home and you scared the boy. Do you never think of anyone but yourself? I don't see what my son saw in you. But love is blind, I guess. Maybe I'm just old fashioned."

Sophie emerged at the bottom of the stairs. She walked to the kitchen and gave a quick glance at Evelyn. Sophie knew if she ever tried anything like Evelyn did, it would be her on the chopping block. She remembered when Winston told her the truth about how his family made a living. She loved him. But at first, she hated the thought of killing for profit. Sophie touched her pearls and shivered.

"What's with that damn necklace?" Evelyn asked.

Sophie's head snapped toward Evelyn. "What do you mean?"

"You're always wearing it. It's annoying. And you're always touching it."

"It was my mother's necklace. My father bought it for her, just because he loved her. And now it belongs to me."

"Did you shoot your mother in the back too?"

Sophie smiled. "You want to hear about this necklace? I'll give you the short version so you don't die half way through it. My parents were controlling. They tried to dictate my entire life. They wanted the best for me. But for some reason, they did not approve of Winston. It didn't matter. I was almost eighteen. I did not need their approval anymore. But I did convince them to have dinner one night here at the Hamilton's. It wasn't long before they too were bleeding out exactly where you lay. My mother couldn't hold her tongue. It's classless to speak ill of a person in their own home."

"You killed your own mother?" Evelyn asked, wheezing with each word.

"No. But I did pick this necklace up off the floor once Winston's father severed her head. It was lying in a pool of her own blood. I was afraid it would stain at first. But I washed it gently and it's been good as new ever since. I touch it to remind myself to never be like her."

Sophie leaned down and whispered into Evelyn's ear so Winston wouldn't hear. "I touch it to remind myself to never end up like her either; on this damn butcher block."

"There's always tomorrow," Evelyn replied,

coughing on her own blood.

"There's no tomorrow for you," Winston said as he walked up next to the butcher block holding his hatchet. "Don't wanna scare the boy again with all your screaming. I guess I'll make this quick," he said, raising the hatchet above his head.

"Melvin! Run!" Evelyn screamed as loud as she could.

One swift movement and the hatchet was brought down across her neck. Winston swung so hard that the blade penetrated through Evelyn and the wood beneath.

Winston's eyes met Sophie's. They embraced one another in a passionate kiss. Their tongues wrestled one another as the blood leaked from both of Evelyn's carotid arteries onto the kitchen floor.

"Grandpa?" Melvin asked. The little boy stood at the bottom of the stairs. He was looking down the hallway into the kitchen. He saw his grandparents kissing and a headless body lying on the kitchen island.

Winston and Sophie both turned around.

"Come here Melvin," Winston told the boy.

Melvin slowly made his way down the hall and

into the kitchen. He looked at the blood on the floor and then his eyes grew big when he noticed his mother's head laying across the room.

"Can you keep a secret?" the old man asked his grandson. The man's face was wrinkled and his cheeks had sunken into themselves where the years had aged his face. The old man was almost completely bald. Only a thin dusting of white hair wrapped around the sides to the back of his head. He bared down into the young boy's eyes and did not blink. The little boy stared into the wild eyes of his grandfather. He knew he had no choice in the matter. What he had just witnessed scared him. Not like a jump scare like in a movie, but a frightful scene that shook the boy to his core. A scene that would haunt him for the rest of his life, however long that may be. It was childhood trauma at its best.

"Ok, Grandpa. I won't tell. Just like in the barn. I promise, I'll be a good boy. I won't say a word."

Winston Hamilton flashed his dentures and smiled a wicked smile, satisfied with his grandson's response. "You're a special boy, Melvin. Now come closer and watch how I do it. I can teach you too." Winston walked back around to the butcherblock countertop. He picked up the hatchet and continued chopping. The sound of metal cutting into bone sank deep into the boy's ears, penetrating his mind. Just as Melvin took a few steps closer to get a better look, the old man swung the hatchet down again. Blood gushed out and splattered onto the boy's face.

"This hatchet was used to help chop wood to build this very house. This hatchet was used to help build the barn. And it's been used to feed the fish. This hatchet is a family heirloom, Melvin," Winston explained to his grandson as he continued to sever limbs from Evelyn's dead body.

Sophie walked behind her grandson and placed her hands on his shoulders. She knelt down beside him and whispered into his ear. "Just mind your manners and this will never happen to you."

Melvin did not speak. He continued to watch his grandfather as he chopped his mother up into pieces right in front of him. At first, Melvin jumped at the sound the hatchet made when it would chop down through the bone. Chop. Chop. Chop. But then he no longer jumped. The sound became intoxicating to listen to. He started to like it.

Sophie picked up Evelyn's head and placed it on the countertop. After all the limbs were detached from the torso, Melvin stood next to his grandmother to watch her.

"Hand me the ice cream scoop," she ordered the boy.

Melvin picked up the metal scoop and passed it to her. Sophie lined the tip of the scoop up with the edge of Evelyn's left eye. One quick flick of the wrist and the eye popped out of its socket. She placed the slimy orb on a metal tray that was lying in front of Melvin. Another flick of the wrist and the second eye popped out with ease.

While Winston was filleting the flesh, Sophie began carving the face off the skull. Melvin took turns watching them both work in silence. He looked at the eyes laying on the tray again. Curiously, the boy picked up one of the eyeballs. He brought it up to his own eye and inspected the squishy orb. Without giving it much thought, he popped the eyeball into his mouth and started to chew.

"Melvin!" Sophie screamed.

Melvin looked up to her, continuing to chew on

the gooey orb. Sophie watched in horror as her grandson chewed and swallowed his mother's eyeball.

"Winston, your grandson just ate an eyeball. What are we going to do about this?" she inquired.

Winston stopped cutting and looked over at Melvin. He looked at the head sitting on the counter with two empty sockets. He looked at the tray behind Melvin with only one eyeball remaining.

"I'm no expert on cannibalism, Melvin. But if you're going to eat people then you better let your grandmother cook the flesh first. Sophie, fry some of this meat up for Melvin. He's a growing boy. We wouldn't want the heir to the Hamilton fortune to get an upset stomach."

Made in the USA
Middletown, DE
03 June 2024